Ten Yen

The Making of a Monk

Christina St. Clair

ISBN: 978-1-62420-103-5

Credits
Cover Artist: Designs by Ms G
Editor: Sherry Derr-Wille

Printed in the United States of America

Dedication

To All Who Are Seeking Love

One

Joumi Kouki barely noticed the makeshift arcades on Ginza Street. Many of the merchants bought goods from him, often illegally. That was how he'd been able to afford to operate his motor car and so much more. War had been an evil but he'd turned its aftermath into profit. He had and would outdo the Americans who had invited him to a reception in the Waco Building where they'd set up a PX. He was not coming here to talk about any products for purchase, under the table or otherwise. Instead, he was invited to a festive time intended to woo the Japanese and turn them into friends.

He drove down a side street and found a parking spot in front of a bar, currently closed. People, perhaps envious of his wealth, stared at him briefly as he shut off the motor and clambered out onto the sidewalk. Few people owned their own cars, let alone a beauty like this one with its white-wall tires, shining chassis, and leather seats. "Boy," Joumi called to a kid who, judging from the state of his ragged clothes was most likely a street urchin. "Here's five yen. You watch my car, and I'll give you another five when I come back."

The boy seized the money and looked slyly at Joumi. "Wanna meet my sister? You take me for a ride?"

Joumi shook his head. "No chance. You'd stain the seats."

People who'd been watching shook their heads. He heard an old woman mutter he ought not to encourage these charinko orphan kids who more often than not were pickpockets. She soon went her way, disappearing into the crowd, tapping the side of her face, and muttering about the shocking state of things. They all wanted to forget the past, himself included, but part of him could not help but grieve for the street kids who had no family to help them. He remembered only too well how bad it felt to be unwanted.

All of their returning soldiers were greeted with scorn. Had they not done what their military leaders dictated? Had they not believed in the holy war to liberate Asia? Surely they could not be blamed. Was it freedom to leave little girls carrying the white sack filled with the ashes of their parents and brothers to fend for themselves? He loved them, his Japanese fellows, stupid sheep though they were, now trying to re-invent themselves, many wearing Western clothes.

He too sported a dark gray suit handmade and shipped to him from London. He knew how to play the Western game better than anyone and wore such clothes not merely out of vanity, but because he knew foreigners sneered at Japanese ways, considering them inferior. No matter how much they pretended to be brothers and liberators, they were first and foremost occupiers with the upper hand.

Joumi made his way through the crowds of people out bargain hunting glad to feel them bump into him, glad of their nearness, so unlike most of the foreigners he'd met who wanted to be isolated from one another. His father, who'd been schooled in England, had tried to be like the English, aloof and unloving, even buying a Georgian-style house here in Tokyo where Joumi had vague memories of his mother. She'd been just the opposite of his father: warm and traditional, always wearing kimono and obi, sporting dainty slippers, and being totally obedient to her husband. The man had *not* adored her, but she'd had a calming influence upon him. He'd gotten meaner after she'd died and often beat Joumi's legs with a cane until he bled. He'd yell at the boy he must be strong, must be a man, and pain was the way to courage.

Joumi used to believe such nonsense and even tried to become a kamikaze, willing to die for Emperor Hirohito, but instead he'd been assigned as a guard in a POW camp here in Japan. He supposed he'd been lucky to escape from the hell of active battle. He'd been sickened by the bombings of Hiroshima and Nagasaki. He'd not been part of the mob who'd dragged the American prisoners out of the camp and beaten them to death as if that could bring back the hundreds of thousands of his people who'd been needlessly slaughtered. He'd known Japan was about to capitulate. Surely their enemies knew it too, but they'd wanted their pint of blood. They'd gotten more than their share, not at all in keeping with the so-called Japanese atrocities against *them*.

But that was then and this was now. The war was over. Five years had passed. Now he must be friends with these Americans whether or not he despised them. His smile became beatific, his eyes deeply cautious, as he noted the time on the clock tower above the Waco Building. He could not help but admire its curved granite façade with its tall windows rising in columns seven stories high, untouched by incendiary bombs.

A Japanese doorman greeted him with a deep bow. Joumi nodded back, his gesture intentionally slight, clearly declaring his superior status. He swept through the doors, taking long strides, walking purposefully, and yet his stomach quivered with dread. He did not enjoy parties. Perhaps he was more like his father than he wanted to admit. Perhaps he was more like those standoffish Englishmen his father had tried to emulate.

People milled around two low-slung tables laden with all manner of foods. He could smell the rice vinegar in the *tamagoyaki* made with eggs and shrimp, a popular breakfast meal, but not something any Japanese would serve in the afternoon. A waiter poured him a glass of saké. He took a sip. This he would certainly relish. He looked over the food tables noting that at least someone had been careful to separate the blue-backed fish from the white-fleshed sushi. All the cuisine on one table was Japanese, whereas all the food on the other was American fare. Hamburgers, hotdogs, macaroni and cheese looked revolting to him.

His face did not show his disgust. He would eat what he chose when he chose. His eyes roamed the people, sizing them up. He saw many American officers in uniform, none of whom he knew, but he did not expect to meet with Sergeant Robinson, the man he dealt with over purchase of illicit goods. He kept his secret smile of satisfaction hidden. He'd been invited by a major he'd met briefly amongst many other foreign military at a discussion about commerce and the rebuilding of Tokyo.

A few Westerners, probably diplomats, in well-cut suits, were sampling *zensai azuki* beans with dumplings. He turned his observations elsewhere not wanting to embarrass these fools who could not appreciate the finesse of good food and who would probably show their squeamishness in obvious frowns or sneers.

There were many women in stylish gowns, but his glance fell upon the bright red kimono on a young woman's back. What attracted his attention wasn't just her dress draped loosely around her slender waist, made from exquisite silk embroidered with cherry blossoms. The quality of the clothing did not particularly excite him, although he was always on the lookout for potentially profitable dresses women could buy. The dress showed off her plump hips, and the way it swept gracefully to the ground appealed to him, but there was something more about *her*. Even though he couldn't see her face, an inner voice said this is *she*. Her shiny black hair pinned up in a bouffant showed off the ends of hairpins fashioned into miniature dragons, made from what must surely be pure silver. He could not stop staring at her delicate back.

At last, as if she could feel his gaze, she turned around. The woman clearly knew he'd been staring at her person. Her eyes sought his. When their look met, she did not smile, and nor did he. He felt lost in her deep gaze, almost giddy. He bowed deeply to her without for one instant taking his eyes away from hers.

~ * ~

Amaya Shimizu wanted adulation but at first ignored the intrusive glare she'd felt. She'd been a little annoyed to go so unnoticed by the Americans who'd greeted her in the grand hall. They'd been cordial but did not seem to understand her success as an actress. It was as if they didn't know, but they must have known else why had she been asked to come? *Except,* she thought ruefully, *the Yank who'd invited her had backed out at the last moment, no doubt because his wife would be accompanying him. How could he introduce them to one another?* Not that Amaya ever considered him anything more than a fling like so many others she'd enjoyed toying with as wantonly as the way her husband used women. She'd pretended to be his obedient wife accepting his bragging about his liaisons with other girls, accepting his drunken homecomings and demands for dinner, but the truth was she'd been jealous, hurt, and horribly demeaned. Had she been able, she'd have divorced him within a year of their wedding day, but she'd been saved the disgrace. It seemed hard to believe seven years had passed since the accident. While inspecting a roof damaged from a bomb, the tiles suddenly caved in, and he'd fallen to his death.

Amaya pivoted away from the table taking a long look at the tall geeky-looking Japanese guy with protruding ears who was gazing at her. His skinny frame would normally have been a turn-off for Amaya. She liked her men well-muscled. But right now she wanted attention and he appeared to be the only person in this gathering willing to give it to her. His eyes however really *were* magnetic. She couldn't look away or even pretend to be shy. *So be myself with him.* He dressed as most successful Japanese did in a suit and tie rather than traditional Japanese attire. How amusing it would be to shock him by coming on to him as if she were one of the many prostitutes who called themselves Geisha to seem exotic to the American invaders. Of course, she'd have to make sure he knew full well that she was an important actress.

It would not do for anyone to find out she had in fact turned briefly to prostitution after WW II ended, but not as one of the thousands of state-run whores who took care of the occupying troops so that *nice* Japanese girls and women would not be molested. Supposedly it helped for a while, but still many women had been raped and murdered with no recourse. Amaya was deeply ashamed of her behavior, but she'd had so little choice. It beat eating acorns and pounding sawdust into an unpalatable powder to mix with flour. She'd managed to ingratiate herself to a wealthy British officer high in the ranks. He'd kept her in an apartment three times the size of the house she'd shared with her parents and three brothers in Hiroshima.

She still lived in the swank flat, and he still paid the rent, which amused her because he was safely back in England with his family and hardly likely to come back to Japan now. His letters, long and effusive, declared her as the love of his life, and lamented his inability to bring her home to England. As if she'd want to go! He bemoaned the fact he simply could not divorce his wife. He had three children to consider. Amaya wrote him discreet letters sent to his office in the Houses of Parliament. She sympathized with his plight, and titillated him just enough to keep him hoping *and* paying.

Amaya came out of her reverie. *Yokatta koto, my goodness,* the Japanese man looked as if he intended to approach her. She needed no patron these days. She was glad when people stepped in front of him and got in his way. Still, she always kept her options open. Amaya slipped past the people, coquettishly lowering her eyes and fluttering her eyelids theatrically. After a suitable interval when she was standing directly in front of the guy, she gaily smiled up into his enthralled eyes. For a moment, saying nothing, she merely sized him up, keeping the pretty smile on her face, strongly aware of his masculine scent. His presence, in spite of his lanky height, reminded her of a samurai. *Better still,* she thought to herself, *he is a Buddha.* He certainly has the ears. "You," she said, reaching a tiny hand toward his lapel, and gently straightening his tie. "I will call you my Ookii Mimi!"

~ * ~

Joumi couldn't help but grin down into her exquisite face. To be nicknamed *Big Ears* seemed quite a complement. He certainly did have some money, as people believed about men with long earlobes but not because he was lucky as they surmised. No. He'd worked hard and ruthlessly to earn every yen. "What might I call you?" he murmured, bowing to her deeply. As he straightened, he intentionally moved closer to her, his hair grazing her cheek. He could smell a faint fragrance of koh and wondered if she burned incense to the gods or had perhaps been recently in a temple. "You are a living incarnation of Amaterisu," he said sincerely.

"You may call me Amaya. That is my real name." She daintily covered her mouth with one hand and giggled. "If we are to be friends, you will soon find out I am not the goddess you wish me to be."

Her face made-up as perfectly as a Geisha was not painted with the traditional white rice powder, but rather glowed with health. He suspected beneath her makeup her skin was healthy brown, perhaps even tanned. "Let me take you to dine somewhere more suitable than this place." He waved his hand dismissively towards the food tables. "Unless you prefer a cheeseburger?"

"I don't even know your name," she responded, enjoying their game.

"I am Joumi, Amaya," he said, tasting her name on his tongue. "If you are to be my Amaterisu, you must indeed call me Ookii Mimi."

"Perhaps." Amaya's eyes gleamed with delight. Did he think she could be bought? Somehow she thought he would not attempt anything so brutish. "Let us go somewhere more private where we can get acquainted properly. My place or yours?"

Joumi hid his surprise. Surely not. Was she propositioning him? *How very flattering*, he thought. "Why, yours," he said, and wished he'd said *his* house, but he did not ever bring women into his spotless home, preferring to fulfill his needs with local prostitutes in Nerima-ku, the last of the twenty three wards recently formed to satisfy the occupiers' intention to turn Japan into a democratic state.

Amaya hid her irritation with this man. He was no big-eared Buddha, holy and beyond physical needs! She couldn't imagine why she'd so impulsively invited him to her flat. Even the men she played around with weren't allowed there. Hotels were good enough for them.

Joumi watched Amaya's sudden look of disappointment, and felt his heart shrivel. He didn't want her to be a high-class prostitute, but perhaps she *was* a Geisha. And if she was, he wanted to give her a chance to say so. "You live in an okiya?" He'd taken wealthy Americans to flower towns where the Geisha houses were found. More often than not, these guys expected more than entertainment. He usually found high-class brothels for them to enjoy.

"Geisha?" she looked momentarily thoughtful, as if trying to decide whether or not to tell him something. "I am not. I make my living acting but perhaps I have something in common with them. I have freedom and am in no need of a benefactor. I am Amaya Shimizu, the actress. I have been in the films of Ozu. Teinosue Kinugasa himself has been my director."

"Ahhh," Joumi murmured. So that accounted for her forward behavior. "My work keeps me too busy to watch movies, but now I will look for you on every banner at every theater."

"Shall we go?" Amaya could not help but be pleased with his infatuation. She placed her hand on his forearm. "My flat is in one of the new apartment buildings in Asakusa. It's not far from here. Shall we call a cab?"

Two

Joumi gave the street boy who'd been keeping an eye on his car a ten yen coin, shooing him away. "Off you go. Don't spend it on cigarettes," he admonished, aware of Amaya watching him without giving a hint of how she felt about his generosity. Perhaps she thought him foolish. He held the car door open for her and helped her into the passenger seat.

Amaya settled herself into the leather seat, adjusting the skirt of her kimono. She watched the scruffy little boy skip away, dodging in and out of people, clearly elated to have 'earned' such easy money. She wondered if Joumi expected to pay her and how much he would offer. It would be tempting to allow him his folly, perhaps even demand an extravagant amount on the brief drive to her place, and then throw the money in his face and tell him to get out of her sight. She threw him a devilish glance. How serious he was. His kindness to the boy did not deserve derision. "Asakusa is a mile or two from here."

"Yes, I know the way." Joumi hit the accelerator. The car roared down the side street a little too fast. He felt embarrassed. He knew he was acting like a silly boy instead of the thirty-year-old man he was. Joumi slowed the car and turned onto another street, leaving behind the many arcades laden with cheap sweaters, some of which he supplied from his American connections. These clothes went for a big profit. He felt guilty about taking advantage of people, but if they could afford such luxuries, then they were not amongst the many selling their possessions to buy food.

As they drove through a shanty town where he rarely went, he wondered why he'd chosen to expose Amaya to such a place. Some intuition told him she was no stranger to hardship, beautiful and exquisite though she seemed. He wondered what had her life been before and since the war? Many residences in Tokyo had been destroyed by the firebombing. These people they passed still lived like paupers settling for canvas-roofed shacks thrown together with any debris they'd been able to find or steal. A child of no more than seven dragged a cart loaded with what looked like the remnants of old rugs. Women sewed them together for blankets and used them to cover the opening of their three-sided huts or laid them on the cold hard floor since it was unlikely they had bamboo mats for sleeping.

Amaya tried to stifle her tiny moan. She couldn't bear to see little children in such dire circumstances. It hurt her to see people struggling in such squalor. There was so little she could do to help. "It was generous of you to give that kid money," she managed.

Joumi glanced at her sideways. "I was paying him for watching over my car."

"It is very handsome vehicle," Amaya said, stroking the leather upholstery. She wanted to ask how he'd come by it, but did not want to insult him. Perhaps he'd always had money, though she suspected not. What aristocrat would pay an orphan to watch a car no one could possibly steal? Most of the people wandering the streets, except the Brits and Yanks, didn't know how to drive anything other than bicycles.

"The car was a present from the Emperor," he muttered sourly, caught up in his usual anger. Her incredulous gasp, though, made his mouth quiver in a smile.

Amaya noticed the upturn of his lips. "You are making fun of me."

"No, no." Joumi wanted more than anything to win her approval. He wanted her to understand why he'd done what he'd done. "Hirohito *was* responsible for my prosperity. After all, he is the one sent us all into war and brought down the wrath of the Americans. That child back there and all those half-starved people living in slums can thank him for his idiocy, him and the warlords who control him."

Amaya hesitated, not knowing how to respond to his outburst of anger. "You should be ashamed," she said at last. "It was not the Emperor's fault we lost the war. We should have tried harder. We let him down."

Joumi groaned. "I suppose you threw yourself prostrate when you heard his speech, that's if you could understand his words. He certainly loves his subjects so much he can't even be bothered to speak intelligible Japanese."

"He is above us. It's natural he should be a classicist."

"What rubbish," Joumi said dismissively. "I'm sorry," he murmured. "I have no right to criticize you for your loyalty. Tell me about yourself."

"My building is nearby." Amaya hid her frown. It had been a mistake to bring him here. The new brick high-rise dominating the landscape seem to touch dark clouds roiling across the sky. Joumi seemed to her as the sort of man who would no doubt disapprove of this modern, clean apartment building. It did not disguise the stink of everyday life, though. The railings around the small balconies in front of the sliding glass doors were laden with laundry out to dry. He, no doubt, in his fancy car, thought himself better than ordinary people.

Joumi glided to a stop in front of an entrance flanked by concrete Imperial dragons. Since it was clearly a Western-style building, he wondered who'd added the dragons. Did they not know these were Chinese symbols? Of course there were Japanese dragons too. He found himself wondering how Amaya had gotten to live in such an expensive place.

Bicycles were scattered against the front wall. He felt immensely grateful that his days of hawking goods no longer required him to pedal furiously from vendor to vendor to chat them up and sell them illegally gotten goods.

He shut off his motor, jumped out, and hurried around to the passenger side to throw open the door. When he tried to help Amaya out of the car, offering her his hand, she took the rim of the chassis and pulled herself upright. She minced toward the building constricted by the slenderness of her kimono. Somehow she managed to walk as fast as an angry mother bear, her head held high, her eyes staring at the ground. In front of the doorway she turned and glared. He felt his spirits shrink, terrified she was about to tell him to go away. If only he could learn to keep his tongue still.

"Joumi," she said. "Just what do you mean Hirohito gave you such a grand car? Are you a gangster?"

"I?" he chortled aloud. "Of course not! Let's just say I have taken advantage of many entrepreneurial opportunities that would not have occurred if our fine Emperor had not capitulated." Yet even as Joumi announced this truth, he wondered if perhaps he *was* a crook, but he'd never murdered anyone, so surely he was no thug? He would, however, willingly slaughter the officers who'd ruled their soldiers through terror. Not that he'd ever experienced such cruelty, but he'd talked with plenty of returning warriors who'd admitted that if they'd had the chance they'd have gladly put a bullet in the brains of their leaders. "My car, as a matter of fact, was given to me by an American friend who returned to his country," he said noncommittally without admitting this 'friend' owed him favors, and silence came at a price.

Amaya's eyes flashed but she did not reveal she too had a foreign friend, not that she cared what Joumi might think of her. "I live on the fifth floor. There is an elevator. Come along. I will serve you tea."

"I think not," Joumi responded, bowing. "I would like to prepare the tea for you." He could not imagine why he had taken this chance. Such an offer to any traditional lady would probably alienate her. He could only hope it would make this woman smile.

But she did not smile. She walked ahead of him, pressed the elevator button and stared at the metal doors until they clattered open. "My father used to make tea for my mother."

Joumi followed Amaya on the elevator and watched her trembling finger push the button for her floor. How sad she'd become.

Amaya got out a key she had tucked in a sleeve and opened her front door. "Please come in." She stood aside to let him enter first.

The moment he saw the low-slung green couch and the fancy upholstered chair placed carefully

18

around a shag rug, he knew what he did not want to know. This woman could not possibly own such things or afford such an apartment unless she was truly a famous and well-paid actress. It was so obviously *not* Japanese, so clearly set up to suit the taste of a Westerner. He was surprised to notice on a shelf the blue and white porcelain mizusashi, clearly a very old water container for a tea ceremony. It seemed out of place with all the modern furnishings and yet he sensed it was something Amaya thought precious, unless she'd positioned it in this sitting-room to charm the mind of someone non-Japanese. Where in the world was *her* loyalty? He knew many people, indeed most people, had all but lost their sense of tradition after defeat. Perhaps her exaggerated Japanese attire was her way of atoning for what seemed obviously a love nest. Yet, oddly, he was not offended. He wanted to rescue her. He took her delicate hand and led her to the couch. "Come," he said. "Sit. While I make tea." He silently regarded the mizusashi.

Amaya stood staring at the couch horribly aware she'd been bedded here by her officer friend more than once and she'd pretended to love him, pretended their sex was exciting, pretended to orgasm. She *had* felt abashed after the Emperor's speech, it was true, but now in this moment, something she'd arrogantly denied as nothing more than a game of survival, became deeply shaming. Her face flushed. She wanted to run away from this tall Japanese, her fellow countryman, and yet she sensed at some level he understood. She reverently picked up the water container, and smiling sadly at Joumi, held it out to him in both her hands almost in the manner of a prayer.

"It belonged to my parents. My father always fetched fresh spring water for our tea." She hesitated. Should she tell him? "We lived in Hiroshima."

Joumi felt himself grow silent, inviting her to speak. Hiroshima did not shock him. He knew now. He waited, nodding his head gently.

"I had to eat acorns," she cried. "I used to mix sawdust with flour. The Emperor did not drop the bombs."

Joumi resisted his temptation to be angry with her naiveté and mention *who* forced the Americans into the war, *who* led their country for years even before that with shameful invasions into Manchuria and China, *who* used up all their resources, leaving the people starving. The grief on her face made him want to take her in his arms. This woman needed to cry. How many people had never cried but instead become zombies without emotion, hardly able to face the next day? He'd been like that for a while after their unconditional surrender.

"My husband," Amaya said, not hiding the disgust on her face, "brought me to Tokyo. After he got killed, I stayed here. I never saw my mother or father again. They are ashes amongst ashes. All of them." She took back the water container and carefully put it back on the shelf. "I do not miss my husband!"

Her voice sounded defiant. "Let us not bother with tea." She did not want him to discover the tin of black oolong she kept in her kitchen, a gift from England. She did not want to have to invent a story. She was sick of lies, perhaps the deepest being that she might yet become a famous actress. He would soon find out if he decided to look for her in the movie theaters that she'd only played minor supporting roles. Her name was on no banners. Her name barely made it on the credits and by the time it was displayed, most of the audience had already left the theater. "Come, let us light the brazier, please. It's next door in the dining room."

Joumi followed her into a smaller room much more pleasing to his taste with its low central table and delicate room divider decorated with plum blossoms. This seemed so much more in keeping with who she really was. Behind the screen, he could see the edge of a sleeping mat. Clearly there was no room for more than one person. His hopes soared. Perhaps she lived and slept here alone.

Amaya knew he'd noticed her bed. Men were so transparent. She motioned to the small heater in the well at the center of the table. "Let us warm some saké and get drunk."

Three

"So," Amaya smiled sweetly at Joumi. "You like your nihonshu heated?"

He nodded, a little astonished at her suggestion they get drunk together. "Yes, it will be good warmed." He was tempted for a lot more than liquor, and in fact did not care for cheap warmed wine having become accustomed to only the best rice wine still fermented the old fashioned way and served cold, unlike these cheap substitutes fortified with glucose and ethanol. But he intended to go along with her wishes. He wanted to savor her much like the savoring of tea at the tea ceremonies. "Just a small drink, then I must go."

Amaya did not show her irritation at this man who thought he could breeze into her life and stay but a few moments. She was glad, though, he was not like so many men who wanted to immediately rip off her kimono, especially the Americans she'd known. She preferred not to remember the behavior of her officer. None of the foreigners had any finesse. Japanese men often wanted *their* women to seductively disrobe. *They* would take their time. She ran her hands down the front of kimono as if to remove any creases, but also seductively. She could create havoc in this self-possessed Big Ears. She could make him beg! "Just a moment," she whispered, her tongue seductively moistening her lips.

Joumi answered with a slight bow but his deep gaze captured her eyes for a moment. He could feel her embarrassment at his eye contact and noticed a flutter in his gut. When she came back with an exquisite porcelain jar and two wooden cups fashioned like antique masu once used for measuring rice, except in miniature, he again wondered about her resources, but he did not want to contemplate the obvious, and decided to treat her as the famous actress she claimed to be. And it could be so. She was beautiful enough.

They sat comfortably side by side on a bamboo mat, leaning their elbows onto the table.

Amaya lit the oil heater in the well in the middle of the table. She leaned forward and held the jar of wine over the flame, swirling it around, heating it only slightly before pouring them each a cup. Her hands on either side of the cup, she tilted the wooden vessel slowly into her mouth, not taking her eyes away from his.

Joumi took a small sip. "This is very good," he couldn't help but exclaim. "Kanpai," he toasted.

"Cheers," she responded wickedly, intentionally remembering *whose* money had paid for this expensive wine, something her long-departed officer continued to insist she must have, often sending her extra cash. In return, she wrote about how she missed being embraced by his big strong arms, which they were, but oh so white and hairy. Her shame at Joumi's pushy eye-contact passed, especially remembering it was *she* using him. She could not help her smile.

"What?" Joumi asked. "What is funny?"

Amaya held a finger to her lips. "It is a secret."

What layers must he peel away to find out about the real Amaya, Joumi wondered, and slowly continued sipping his drink. "So," he said. "So..."

"I am from Hiroshima," Amaya watched him for his reaction. When she'd mentioned it before he had not looked away out of sorrow as so many people did. Some responded from fear too as if they thought she might contaminate them with the radiation that had killed many innocent people, including all in her family except her brother, Haruo.

"You told me." Joumi looked at her steadily. Should he ask her about her kinfolk? He'd waited for her to tell him more before and she'd skipped away from the subject. "I have never been there. It must have been beautiful."

Amaya's eyes became distant. "When I was a

little girl, I used to go to the river and play beneath the Aioi Bridge. My parents forbade it, but I knew I was safe near that lovely green water. I liked to throw in sticks and watch them float away underneath the bridge columns. I sometimes was naughty and threw pebbles at boats, but I never hit any. Sometimes people waved to me." She blinked back moisture. "I still remember the rumble of the trolley cars crossing above me on the bridge."

Joumi hardly dared speak. She spoke about geography but not about family. He knew what it meant. He also knew this bridge, famous because it was shaped like a T, had been the target for the atomic bomb and yet had somehow survived even though it was close to the epicenter of the bomb blast. Perhaps her people had survived too. "The bridge is not gone," he whispered.

"No," Amaya said as if reading his mind. "At least that is so. None of my folks except my brother lived through it. I was not there. My husband is at least to be thanked for bringing me to Tokyo or I too would be dead."

"I am glad you are still here." Joumi picked up the jar of wine. "Come. Let us celebrate that we live on."

Amaya did not feel like celebrating, but she gladly drank another glass of wine to take away the chill in her heart. And another and another. Before long she was giggling. She threw herself sideways, landing on Joumi's feet. "Ha ha ha," she mocked him.

"You have big feet as well as big ears."

He grabbed her shoulders and set her upright, but she rocked sideways again and began to laugh so hard he began to laugh too.

Amaya liked his deep voice and she liked his gentle hands. "I am going to change into something comfortable," she said, crawling behind the screen. She managed to pull herself upright and began to strip off her clothes, first removing her obi and slinging it outside of the screen so he could see it. After she slipped out of her kimono, letting it fall to the floor, she stretched her arms high in the air and arched her back, aware her flat belly and perfect breasts would be visible through the screen.

Joumi watched her taking off her clothes. Her slender body behind the paper panels looked ghostly, silver, exquisite. He knew she meant for him to see. He did not want her this way. Joumi went into the Western sitting room and sat on the couch. The saké had made him sleepy. What would he say to her if she expected sex with him? He wasn't going to do it. Not now. His head fell forward on his chest. He began to dream.

He rode a giant red-crowned crane of peace high in the sky above Tokyo. Below him he could see a boy with dark eyes in monk's clothing leaning over a very old man who seemed near to death. The dying man must be a monk too, but who was this boy? Another boy flashed before his eyes—a bald English child with gentle eyes. The two seemed to merge.

"No," he shouted, jolting awake.

"No what?" Amaya leaned over him, now wearing blue monpe pantaloons, so baggy around her hips she looked even tinier. The long sleeves of her flowered silk shirt brushed across him as she climbed onto his lap. "No?" she said seductively and tried to put her lips against his, but he turned his head away.

Still half asleep, Joumi babbled what seemed meaningless. "No, I will not die. You cannot kill me. This child cannot perform the task. He is too young to understand. I will not die." He gripped Amaya's wrist so hard it hurt.

"You," she shouted, leaping up away from him. How dare he hurt her! How dare he play hard to get! Her mood sank low and weepy in spite of the booze and perhaps because of it too. She wanted him to hold her, to comfort her, and fill the emptiness inside. "You," she groaned. "You get out of here. I never want to see you again." She tugged on his arm to raise him to his feet, but he grabbed her around her waist and pulled her against his chest. "Amaya, hush, hush," he whispered. "It will be okay."

Joumi suddenly noticed she'd washed off her makeup and brushed out her hair. The gleaming black tresses fell just below her shoulders. She smelled of soap and toothpaste. "How old are you?" he asked, letting her go, scared she might be no more than fifteen.

"I am no longer young," she said, her voice changing and sounding like that of an old woman. In the middle of the room, she began to speak slowly, precisely. "The river boiled. My sons are dead. Where is their chichi? Where is shujin? He will know what to do." Amaya stared at the floor and wailed. "Why does my back hurt so much? Am I burned? Will I be scarred forever?"

Joumi listened in horror as she relayed dreadful accounts of headless bodies, and children burned from head to toe. She described in detail the charred remains of a tricycle. She sounded crazy but not crazy either because he knew what she said was the truth about the town she came from. He could not stop his eyes overflowing with tears. At last she stopped her recitation and when she bowed, he realized she'd been acting. He put his hands together and tried to applaud, but too overcome with emotion, all he could do was clap once.

"A few months after Hirohito gave up, I went to find my parents. I dared to hope they were alive. There was nothing. Our house was gone. Everything shattered. Houses, schools, shops, bridges, all broken to pieces. I'd thought the firebombing of Tokyo hell, but this was far worse. How can anyone describe the complete devastation, and it wasn't only buildings, it was the minds and bodies of the people too. I don't know what stopped me from killing myself. But the mountains still rose above the ruins and the river still flowed. What could I do but come back here and try to live? The oleander is blooming now, so I've been told. I am soon going to see for myself."

"No. You must not. It is still not safe there."

"Radiation does not frighten me. I cannot bring back my family or my neighbors or my friends, but I can go and cheer the little ones in hospitals. Many of them are very sick, you know. They throw up and are skeletons unable to take in nourishment. There are old men and women with no limbs who must be spoon fed. They would rather be dead but now they endure night after endless night of helplessness. I will tell them stories to amuse them. Not like this one I have told you. No, I'll sing for them and play the shamisen. It's not much but it's all I can do to help them remember when their lives were better, when we were all better. So now you know." She turned her back away from him. "I want you to leave, please."

Joumi stood up aware once again of how tiny and frail she was now that she was no longer covered with traditional attire. He knew too she'd revealed deep wounds and she might well never want to see him again because he'd become a mirror of her grief. "Someday I will make you smile," he said quietly, bowing and slowly letting himself out of her flat. As he stood waiting for the elevator, he expected to hear her weeping, but silence pierced his ears like a dagger.

Four

Amaya held the letter from Ben Briton up to the light. The blue stamp in the right-hand corner featured a crown and the image of some British king. The wavy cancellation marks made Amaya sad. This missive was not as thick as usual. Had Ben cut off her money supply, she wondered.

Perhaps it no longer mattered. Perhaps Joumi with his big ears would become her guy. She would become onrii wan—only one—to him. Truly. Her usually pale face flushed, as she thought how often she'd *not* been the onrii wan to Ben like he thought, and though she did not accept money like her friend she fondly called Ginza Girl because she loved to shop, she too could just as easily have become a pan pan selling herself to any GI with money to pay.

Amaya took the letter into her sitting room and squatted next to the table. She'd made herself a pot of tea and poured herself some of the steaming liquid, intentionally using a delicate cup decorated with images of bamboo. She wanted to distance herself from Ben's foreignness, and did not want to be what she knew she'd been to him. After a while, lost in memories she'd have preferred to abandon forever, she slit the letter open with a knife, and took out the fine parchment. There were no pound notes which she usually exchanged for yen. Ben's writing looked less than his neat and measured style as if he'd been in a hurry. She began to read, her eyebrows raised.

"No." She slammed the paper onto the table. "No."

Staring into space, she considered her options. Ben's wife was divorcing him because the fool had taken Amaya's letters home and not hidden them well enough. Perhaps Amaya could write to Lucy Briton, tell her she, Amaya, did not love Ben, and had never loved him, and that he was a fool to think otherwise. Perhaps she could tell Lucy he'd wanted to stay with his wife for the children and probably still did. Perhaps she could teach Lucy how to beguile her husband in new, more exciting ways.

She knew writing to Lucy Briton would not help to keep the woman's husband in England. This wife had no doubt had enough of him. He'd probably opened his mouth and told his wife his plans. The silly man intended to come to Japan to be with her, to marry her, Amaya.

Perhaps she could send him a *Dear John* telling him she would marry no one. No one. Her acting career was taking off and she did not wish to see him again.

Amaya stared into space, sipping her tea until it was cold.

How horrible she felt.

It had been one thing to feed Ben's fantasies and titillate him sexually. That had made *him* feel good. She'd been grateful for the money, for him saving her from the life of a pan pan, for keeping her in this swank apartment, but she had never wanted to break up his marriage. The poor children! They did not deserve to be hurt. But what could she do?

She got wearily to her feet. She must consult with Ginza Girl. Her friend understood men. She would find the solution that would not hurt Ben too desperately and perhaps not dry up the stream of income Amaya needed until she really did become an established actress. She had an audition in a few days with Ozu. It had been a lie she'd told Joumi when she'd said she'd been in this important film director's films, but it hadn't been completely untruthful. She might yet be one of his stars. If he liked her and she got a role in his latest film, she would need no one but herself.

Her journey to her friend's house took her across Tokyo past the Palace Castle, much of it in ruins from the firebombing. She wondered if the emperor sorrowed over the loss of the old palace and if he would ever be able to rebuild. Could any of them ever rebuild lives shattered by war, she thought ruefully. Things were certainly getting better, but no one could bring back her family. No one could give health to the people who'd been hurt because of the war. The Americans told them repeatedly the old ways were archaic and needed to be changed, people needed to think for themselves. They'd even given women the vote.

Amaya hummed the tune to *Big Sunset, Little Sunset*, a song she'd loved as a girl, but now she sang it with the cynical lyrics, *Big Marketeer, Little Marketeer*, reminding her of Joumi. He'd said he wasn't a crook, but who *would* tell the truth? She felt a little lost for a moment, but she sat tall in her trolley seat. She, like everyone else, substituted laughter at themselves for the overwhelming depression wrought upon them by their downfall. How horrified everyone had been to learn of the government asking young women to give themselves to the Americans. How scared and ashamed they'd all been. Ginza Girl said GIs were just guys wanting to get laid like any men might, and some of them were good Joes who gave her chocolates and nylons. Too, it was not true as many thought that these men had overly large dicks that impaled women. Still, some girls did not last a day as prostitutes. Others committed suicide. Yet quite a few made the best of the opportunity. Perhaps they even liked what they did because at least they had the freedom married girls never used to have. She knew all about that. Many pan pans though, later on during the occupation, were arrested by the police who probably felt impotent upon seeing *their* women selling themselves to the Americans.

From the trolley Amaya glimpsed one of the moats of the palatial estate. At least this looked tranquil and clean. An orange and blue kingfisher flitted across the water, landing on one of the rocks at the edge. Amaya wished she might be possessed of wings to take her away from the mess she feared would happen if Ben *did* actually show up. Soon, her bus arrived on Girl's street and she disembarked. Since it was afternoon, she didn't expect her friend to be busy, but she hesitated before climbing the wooden steps to the small room where her friend lived. She knocked and called, "Girl, it's only me. You home? You decent?"

The door slid open and Girl grinned out at her. "Ahh, beek-koo-ree-shee-tah. *What a surprise.*" She bowed slightly and ushered Amaya into her room. It was plush enough with a large American bed in one corner, and her kitchen/dining room behind a screen in another corner. Girl plopped down next to her low table and grabbed Amaya's hand, drawing her onto the nearby mat. "You here for your lessons?" she asked. "I'll turn you into a first rate Geisha, plucking three strings of shamisen so sweetly men will melt." It was a joke between them that they could have become important Geisha women who knew how to play music, recite plays, and hold conversations with wealthy men. Yet they were both grateful they had *not* been sold by their parents to one of many Geisha houses. They were victims of circumstances too but they told themselves they'd been given opportunity and choice.

Amaya went along with their usual games. "I am already Geisha of a great man who took my virginity for very big price."

"I know," Girl said and giggled, hiding her face partly behind a paper fan she'd picked up from the table. "Why, I sell my virginity every day." She set aside the fan and sighed. Without her bright red lipstick on she looked more like a school girl than a woman of the night. "Amaya, you have a very long face. What's wrong?"

Amaya took the letter out of her bag and read it, translating it into Japanese. "What am I to do? I don't want to marry him. I will never go to England. I have an audition in a few days." She did not mention her fantasies about Joumi.

"So tell him, GI piss off!" Girl grinned. "I say it all the time."

Amaya shook her head. "Ben is not a GI. He is in love with me."

"Sure, sure. I met a guy the other day wanted to take me home to Oklahoma and make me a good woman. You know what I told him?"

"Piss off!" Amaya shouted, proud of her friend's fiery nature.

"No. I said he could send for me once he gets home and maybe I'll come. Of course I won't go."

"But Ben is coming here," Amaya cried. "It's my fault. I led him on. I took his money."

"So what. You don't owe him anything."

Amaya thought this over. "I feel as if I *do* owe him for the money he's sent all this time. How can I tell him to piss off? I don't want to hurt him. What about his kids?" Amaya winced at the thought of how bad it ached to lose the ones you loved. Forever. Except Haruo. He was another story she didn't want to think about. "I got an audition with Ozu. What if I don't get a part? What if Ben comes and I send him away? I'll be evicted from my apartment. I'll be out on street."

"You don't want to move in with me?" Girl said, making big eyes, pretending to be hurt. She squeezed Amaya's hand. "It's okay. I understand. I don't want to live with me. Find yourself another guy and become an onrii wan to him."

"I've met a Japanese guy. Joumi Kouki. I think he likes me." Amaya choked up, not wanting to be a kept woman, especially not by Joumi. She wanted him to respect her. Seeing Girl's mouth drop open in astonishment, she felt confused. "You know Joumi?"

"Not personally. I know of him. He's famous around these parts for being the man who ripped off a cache of diamonds from some rich woman killed during the bombings. Some say he stole the jewels from the Imperial Palace right when Hirohito was making his speech of surrender. Myself, I don't believe it. How do you know him? He could be a nice sugar daddy for you."

"If only Ozu decides to hire me as his leading lady, I won't have to worry."

"Kanojo," Girl said. "Girlfriend, don't burn any bridges yet."

~ * ~

Joumi wasted no time investigating Amaya's acting prospects. It came as no surprise to him to learn she was not a big star and in fact had only had a couple of minor roles. This did not concern him, but the fact she lived too well bothered him more than he liked to admit. His sources revealed she'd once had a British lover, a guy called Ben Briton, who'd long since left Japan. Unless Amaya had some other source of income, this guy must still be sending her money. Joumi smiled wryly. He too wanted to keep a connection to lovely Amaya, and it wasn't only her physical beauty he admired. Her kindness, revealed by her wish to go to Hiroshima to help those in need, softened his heart too. Her intelligence, albeit somewhat naïve, pleased him too. Clearly she liked kids and he too hoped for children who would inherit his wealth once he'd established himself as a respectable businessman. Amaya might have resorted to detestable means in order to survive, but who hadn't? He already loved her and he wanted to help her.

When he learned she had an audition with Ozu for a new movie called Tokyo Story, he tried to get a meeting with the guy, but couldn't get an appointment. It became clear to Joumi this director fellow couldn't be bribed. Perhaps he didn't need money or he might just be a principled son-of-a-bitch like Yamaguchi Yoshitada, a judge whose ethics hadn't done him much good since they caused his death. The man had been Joumi's age, thirty, with a wife and kids. He'd judged cases of black marketeering, not of the bigwigs who deserved to go to jail, or even of the sellers, but of ordinary people trying to survive. There'd been one old woman who'd lost her son and her daughter-in-law was dead too. The old woman had, like so many, sold her kimonos so she could afford black market food for her grandkids. Since she was a repeat offender, Yamaguchi had no choice but to send her to jail. It must have made him so sick inside. He decided to abide by the law he'd enforced. Not a complete ass, he allowed his wife, like everyone else, to resort to the black market to feed the children. He, however, starved to death. Plenty of other people continued to starve in spite of this man's self-sacrifice, so what good did it do?

Joumi bashed the rung of the chair with the heel of his shoe. Dining in a swank restaurant with a few other well-to-do businessmen, a couple of government officials and some Americans made Joumi feel guilty. They ate too much, drank too much, and taught the Yanks bawdy songs about hot girls. To him this was all part of the job of keeping money flowing his way in the form of favors, but he hated it as much as he despised having to ask anyone for help—like good old Robinson, now living in New York. He'd phoned his former GI connection convincing him the future held great possibilities for Suminoe Works which had a car prototype called the Flying Feather. Joumi loved cars, and so did Robinson. These light weight Japanese vehicles would be so cheap people world-wide would buy them. Robinson promised to send him a few thousand dollars from the diamond money to invest in the automobile business. He wanted twenty percent of Joumi's profits.

"Sooo," Joumi muttered. "Anyone know Yasujirō Ozu? I want to meet the guy."

"You planning on becoming an actor!" laughed one of the yanks, a captain, with a big nose and a droopy blond mustache that gave his face the look of a hound.

One of the government men held out his hand. "Ten thousand yen will get you a seat in the theater for when they select the actors."

"You're out of your mind," Joumi responded, arching one eyebrow. He couldn't admit he wished to be present when Amaya auditioned. That would certainly give them a good laugh at his and *her* expense. Too many good-looking women could be bought for a hot meal or a pair of nylons. Besides, Joumi certainly didn't want to sit through days if not weeks of hopefuls trying out. "I'm looking for a girl or two," he said with a sly grin. "Who'd be willing to play with my shamisen."

This brought a roar of laughter along with another round of saké.

By the end of the evening, as they stumbled drunkenly out of the restaurant, a guy who'd not said much grabbed Joumi by the elbow. "You tell them Cohen sent you. They'll let you in for free. Guaranteed."

Joumi doubted the man's name was Cohen, a viceroy for MacArthur, but he laughed politely. "You must be very important."

A few days passed when he read in the paper about actresses trying out for parts.

Even though it was drizzling, Joumi walked to the theater with quick jaunty steps. He looked forward to seeing Amaya again. He'd wanted to go to her flat many times but had resisted, biding his time, planning how to woo her. Outside the theater, a doorman stood bowing to passersby. Joumi bowed deeply to the man, trying to ingratiate himself. "I would like to go in and watch the selection process," he said meekly.

The doorman looked him up and down, clearly taking in his expensive clothes. "I'm sorry, sir," the man said with a slight raise of his eyebrows and a subtle flutter of the fingers on his right hand.

Joumi took out a hundred yen. Perhaps the guy wanted a bribe. "Please accept a small token from me for your family as a thank you for being an honest fellow and protecting the virtue of our young actresses. One of them, Amaya Shimizu, is the sister of a friend who died in the conflict. I promised to take care of his little sister. I understand your reluctance."

"Ah, this gets you admission into the gallery. Please to go there and be quiet." He put the money in his jacket pocket and held the door open. "I will escort you."

Joumi sat in the front row of the balcony, which was in darkness so he could not be seen. He was too far back to get a good look at the actresses parading across the stage, but he could hear well enough. Amaya's voice sounded like music. He wanted to applaud when he heard her asked to stay on, not as leading actress but for a part as a hotel maid. It would not pay much and she would almost certainly need more money. All he need do was find a way to get rid of her absent British patron. How hard could that be, he wondered, except what if she loved the guy? Joumi groaned inside.

Outside on the street, the rain had become a steady downpour forcing Joumi to wait in an alcove at the back of the theater, hoping to spy Amaya when she left. He didn't know how he'd explain his presence if she noticed him, but he could always feign coincidence. Or maybe he would follow her and brush past her and pretend to be surprised. He shrugged at his folly. He did not want her to fear him nor did he want a relationship with her based on lies. He'd had enough of them for a lifetime.

After a while, the stage door opened, and people began coming out. As soon as he saw her slender figure, dressed in a tight blue kimono, he couldn't help himself: he stepped out of the shadows into the rain. "Amaya."

She stopped and stared at him. "What are you doing here?"

"I came to see you audition. I was up in the balcony."

"Then you know I got a part." With that she burst into tears. "I wanted a major role. What am I going to do now?"

Joumi wanted to comfort her, but didn't dare for fear she'd think him taking advantage. He took hold of her shoulders and raised her weepy face to his. "This is a start for you. There will be much more. Give it time."

She momentarily collapsed against him. "Yes," she murmured. "Rehearsals don't start for a few weeks. There is plenty of time."

Enjoying the feel of her leaning against him, although he noticed an odd intonation to her voice, he did not ask her what she meant by there being plenty of time. "Please, let me buy you a meal. To celebrate."

Her luminous eyes looked sadly into his. "Yes. Very well. Let us go and celebrate my good fortune."

Five

Joumi hurried around to hold the car door open for Amaya. She accepted his hand and allowed him to help her out. As they made their way into an expensive restaurant, she tucked her little hand in his arm. Inside, away from the noise of the street, the restaurant seemed quiet. It had gleaming wooden floors, low narrow tables with red cushions for seating, and elegant white panels over the windows. People sat talking quietly, enjoying their meals. They could smell salmon and roasted sesame seeds. Joumi licked his lips, feeling hungry for more than good food. He was immensely proud to be with Amaya, dressed as she was in a deep blue silk kimono with wide figured sleeves. Heads turned as they were seated.

Amaya smiled sweetly and seemed completely at ease as Joumi ordered sushi for them both. She ate daintily, clearly appreciating the fine cuisine. He watched her, not wanting to talk, not wanting to spoil her enjoyment of the food. At last, she set aside her chopsticks and gazed into his eyes. He dared to hope there was a magnetic connection between them, but she suddenly looked away, blushing like a girl. She covered her face with her fan, and he knew she was trying to hide, but not from him. He heard the restaurant door slide shut and he looked over his shoulder. Upon seeing an American officer with his wife, Joumi felt a little surprised. "Do you know them?" he asked.

"No." Amaya, startled to see a man who looked very much like Ben, fanned her face, clearly agitated. "He reminds me of someone, that's all." She soon realized upon closer observation that this man was much coarser in build and older too. She still felt panicky and wanted to leave immediately, but did not want to spoil Joumi's evening. He was so generous, and she was beginning to find him more and more attractive.

"Who does he remind you of?" Joumi was certain he knew. It had to be Briton.

"It doesn't matter," Amaya said, dismissively, trying not to show her anxiety. She realized how she was constantly fearful Ben would show up. She wished she had written him a letter telling him to keep away. Amaya decided she would write such a letter as soon as she got home.

Joumi watched her, aware of her agitation. He knew with certainty Ben Briton *had* been sending money on a regular basis. A contact in a bank told him she used to regularly cash in pounds for yen. Joumi made up his mind. He would outdo this guy in every possible way, including, in time, sexually. This thought caused his mind to wander into fantasies about undressing Amaya and all he would do to stimulate her and turn her into mush at his touch. He would make her long for him and want him as much as he wanted her. It would never be enough, though, for it to be merely sensual. He wanted a deep relationship with this woman, and he wanted to be certain she loved him in return and was not playing him in the manner he assumed she must be playing Briton.

"Look," she exclaimed in a delighted voice. "They have taiyaki for dessert." Her eyes glowed. "Do you think I might have one?"

"You shall have as many as you like," beamed Joumi, forgetting his jealousy, wanting only to please her. He decided he would buy a large box of them and take them to her flat very soon.

A memory took away Amaya's delight. Her mother used to buy these fish-shaped cookies specially for her and Haruo. Her little brother used to break open the waffle crust and lick out the sweet bean paste. She wondered how he was and for the first time admitted to herself how afraid she'd been about going to see him. "My brother is alive," she blurted to Joumi, needing to confide in someone but afraid once he knew how she'd deserted the lad, he'd be repulsed by her.

Joumi nodded slowly, wondering at her concerned look. "You are fortunate. I had two sisters who got killed in the firebombing. My brother was killed in the Battle of Okinawa." Joumi felt a pang of grief, something he'd long buried and been unwilling to allow to surface.

"That's terrible," she cried. "But sometimes death is not so bad."

"Let's talk about living, not dying." It was Joumi's turn to be dismissive. His display of emotion embarrassed him. "Kabuki-za Theater is almost ready to open again. Would you enjoy going to a play? Have you ever seen Orochi the eight-headed serpent?"

"Yes, I suppose so. It is very old-fashioned." Amaya felt as did many Japanese people that these ancient myths acted only by men to the sound of shoulder drums and flutes were a waste of time, nothing but a return to an archaic past no one wanted back. She especially disliked the idea of a princess being sacrificed to appease a horrid creature. She felt as if she'd been sacrificed herself, and she didn't want a champion to save her. Amaya wished she had not revealed anything to Joumi about her brother. If he did not want her after he knew the truth, then why should she care? "My brother is fifteen years old now," she said, deciding to ignore his attempt to make small-talk. Who needed chit chat? She didn't want it. "His name is Haruo. He was so badly burned he lost his legs and arms and is now confined to a bed in a hospital in Hiroshima. He cannot talk and is probably fed through a tube." Amaya examined Joumi's startled face. "Now you know," she said. "I am a heartless sister. I have not bothered to return to Hiroshima in five years even when I heard he'd survived." With that, Amaya stood, and nodded curtly at Joumi. "I must go. I am sorry to have misled you about my character. I will call a taxi."

"Wait." Joumi grabbed her hand and half arose.

Amaya did not want to make a scene and sank back onto her cushion by the table aware of the sensation of Joumi's hard grip upon her hand. She stared at their hands.

Joumi released her. He did not know what to think of this revelation. "So that is why you wanted to go to Hiroshima to help," he muttered almost to himself, but he didn't believe it. Amaya was not as giving as he'd wanted to believe. More than likely she'd made up such fantasies to assuage her guilt.

Amaya stared into space. "I am not what you think, the answer to some male dream of yours," she said a little viciously. She almost wanted to tell him about Ben but managed to curb her tongue.

The expression on his face grew stony and cold. "You!" he shook his head, wondering why he felt so disillusioned with her behavior, but in his heart if he did but admit it, he knew the reason. She had abandoned her brother who'd been in need. The loss of all Joumi's family felt like abandonment to him. "You," he began again, "are not to blame for the plight of your brother.

The yanks are the ones who created this misery." He shrugged at the nearby Americans. They probably didn't understand what he'd said, and he didn't care if they did. He'd had enough pandering to them in order to survive, and even though he'd eventually thrived, it wasn't merely because of their help. He really didn't need them anymore, except perhaps for Robinson, but even he could be disregarded. What could the Yank do to Joumi if Joumi chose to keep his investment money and not give him a penny of the profits from the Flying Feathers?

Amaya looked at him shrewdly. His words excused her, but she could feel the doors on his heart shut. She wanted him all the more. She realized she was in love with him. But what could she do to make him love her? He had been very old-fashioned in the way he'd courted her, and he'd never laid a finger on her so it would do no good for her to try to seduce him. It would make him despise her all the more. "I am sorry to have let you down," she said humbly, meaning it, despairing at her own weakness.

He nodded. "It would not be wise for you to go to Hiroshima anyway," he said, still trying to find a way to excuse her. "You must not expose yourself to radiation poisoning."

In that moment, Amaya decided she *would* go to Hiroshima, and she would try to comfort the wounded by playing them a few tunes on the shamisen. She'd practice until she was confident and able to play and sing patriotic songs they'd be bound to enjoy. There was no sense in telling Joumi her plans. He wouldn't believe she was sincere and he'd try to stop her anyway. What if he chose to have nothing more to do with her? She almost burst into tears, but fearful it would seem like a woman's wile to him, managed to blink back her worry.

Joumi summoned the waiter and ordered a plate of taiyaki and some rice cakes.

They sat awkwardly in silence until their dessert arrived. Joumi held out the plate of sweets to her, but she pushed it away. "I can't eat these now. You don't understand. I know I should have taken care of Haruo. I thought about trying to bring him to Tokyo but how could I move him without money, and," she looked away as she said the next words, "my acting roles did not pay me much."

Joumi shrugged, and glared at her. "When did you begin acting? Was it during the time your British lover lived with you?"

Amaya froze. "How do you know this? Who has said this about me? It is a lie! I do not have to listen to such accusations!" But she couldn't bring herself to leave. Instead, she desperately tried to decide if she should reveal the truth to Joumi, but his anger at her filled her with indignation. Had *he* been so good? Had *he* been innocent? "What about *you*?" she spoke haughtily. "*You*, I suppose, have been perfect. I heard you made your money through the black market which is illegal and has broken the backs of many innocent people. I heard too that you stole diamonds and that is why you are now rich." She stared at him defiantly.

Joumi gritted his teeth. "My business is my business. You should not listen to gossip."

"Nor should you," she countered.

Joumi considered should he reveal to her he'd had her investigated. Or would it be wiser to pretend he did not have the facts? No woman wanted to admit she'd been kept by their former enemy. It might make her hate him. Disappointed and confused as he felt, he did not want her to refuse to ever see him again because he'd become a reminder of her immodesty. "I apologize," he said, and bowed over the table. "Let us go and get a drink somewhere and forget this argument. We have both probably done things we regret and cannot change."

Amaya's heart lightened a little. She knew he was angry with her, but her temper had subsided. "Joumi," she said softly. "I will never stop regretting this awful war and what it did to all of us, but at least there are good things happening too. You are someone I want in my life." Her smile brightened her face. "I hope we will always stay friends."

"Of course," Joumi replied, pleased at her remark, and once again wanting much more than mere friendship. He wanted to tell her he loved her, and he wanted to go back to her apartment and hold her and make love to her, but he wasn't ready yet. He wanted her to need him desperately. Then, he might confide some of his shady dealings, but not unless he felt she could be trusted. Regretfully he didn't think she could be relied upon to keep such information quiet. She might even find such knowledge useful and try to exploit him. His ardor cooled. He realized he too wanted to confess and release the burdens on his soul, and that's what she'd been trying to do too by telling him about her brother. She wanted to be forgiven because she couldn't forgive herself. "You are very special to me, Amaya. I want much more than to put you on a pedestal. I want you to become a famous actress if that is what you most want, and I will do my best to help you succeed. I want nothing in return."

Amaya smiled faintly, unable to believe anyone in this world did anything without wanting something in return, including the most well-meaning people.

Joumi paid their bill, and they found a bar displaying a red lantern not far away. Inside they ordered beers. Joumi offered his glass of lager to Amaya and she took a little sip and made a slight face at how bitter it tasted. She'd gotten a small glass of low malt happoshu, which she offered to him.

"It smells like soap." He smiled, taking a swig and swirling it around in his mouth. "Very nice," he murmured, feigning enjoyment.

"Liar." She laughed. "Kanpai." She did what she and Ben always did when they shared a drink, she chinked her glass against his, not knowing this was a British tradition.

Joumi observed her silently, looking over his glass. "Cheers," he said in English, instantly regretting this faux pas.

Amaya did not show how flustered he'd made

her feel. She spoke English but rarely used it. His use of this toast probably meant nothing. It was a common enough expression. Surely, he could not know much about Ben. What had he said earlier? She finished her beer quickly and soon drank another one, matching Joumi brew for brew until she felt quite tipsy in spite of her beer being nowhere near as strong as his. After a while she couldn't stop giggling at how serious he looked. "You are a gangster, aren't you?" She hiccupped.

Joumi did not like to see her drunk, and he did not appreciate another reminder of a past he was putting behind him. He wanted to tell her to shut up, but instead added yet another remark that could only upset her. "Soon the ban on travel is to be lifted. You'll be able to travel to England."

Amaya's face turned whiter than her makeup. She looked down. "I will never go to England," she declared. "Never!"

"Time to go home," Joumi said, slurping the remainder of his beer and settling up with the bartender.

He drove her home and escorted her to the front door of her flat. She leaned against him, a little off balance. "Come in, Joumi, please," she pleaded.

He smiled briefly into her eyes. "Not yet," was all he said, leaving her frustrated and disappointed and wanting him all the more.

Six

Amaya began to relax and enjoy life. Joumi was a perfect gentleman often taking her out for dinner. It was as if he realized she didn't have a lot of money, and wanted to share his wealth. At times she wondered if he were happy since he was so circumspect with her. She'd heard nothing from Ben, and thanked the gods for that. She'd enjoyed her role in the Ozu film thrilled to have been highly praised and recommended for other roles. She'd begun to hope she might earn enough money to need help from no one.

After she landed another part in a film, even though it was only as a supporting actress, she wanted to dance. She had quite a few more lines and was getting to go on location for some of the scenes in the hot spring village of Kurokawa. When the day came for her to leave, she was sad as her train chugged out of Tokyo Station to wave goodbye to Joumi. Once filming was completed, she'd get to see him for a special overnight excursion which she dared hope would be filled with unspeakable delights. Her life couldn't be more perfect. After their time together, filming would resume in the city of Kyoto.

In spite of the hard seat on the train and not getting a window seat, the travel to Kurokawa filled her with happiness by getting away from the city with its noise and over-crowded streets. Once off the train after hours of monotony, where she'd read and re-read her lines, she happily caught the bus to the hot spring town, not minding having to lug her own cases, smiling broadly at the other passengers.

The first sight of Kurokawa filled her pleasure. Steam rose from a hot spring partially covered by a red pagoda roof. A waterfall gurgled over nearby rocks. Pine trees greened and scented the air. "Oh. Beautiful," she remarked to the woman sitting next to her, who nodded.

The bus dropped her off directly outside the guest house where she was staying. Although she couldn't wait to meet the other actors, that evening she recused herself to read the script again. She'd brought a pack of rice cakes and cold noodles for her supper. Her role as the unspoiled young daughter, Eiko, of an innkeeper suited her. She wished *she* could once again be so innocent. The main character, played by a handsome well-known actor, Ebisu, was a real rat who seduced the young girl with no pangs of remorse.

The following day chaos exploded in the village. People swarmed everywhere with cameras and microphones getting ready for the filming. Local people gathered to watch. Amaya and the other actors were introduced, advised what to do, and then it began.

"Shoot," the director commanded. The whir of a camera sounded.

Amaya, acting as Eiko, looked up into the eyes of Ebisu. It was easy to pretend being in love with him. She'd faked it for Ben Briton whom she'd tried to put completely out of her mind and hoped she might truly forget. In fact, just before coming to Kurokawa, she'd overcome her reluctance to permanently cut off the easy money he provided, not that there had been any recently. In any case, she'd written to Ben explaining their time together was over, and he needed to make things up with his wife. He would get her missive while she was away and that should put an end to his fantasies. She'd even scolded him about the very idea of leaving his children, causing her a pang of remorse about her brother, Haruo. She promised herself as soon as the movie ended, she would follow through with her plans to go to Hiroshima.

The filming went smoothly and within three weeks they were winding up. Her very last scene as Eiko completed this phase of the movie-take. Ebisu held her in his arms. "Eiko," he moaned her stage name. "I want you so much, but I must return to my wife. She is unable to take care of herself, but let me make love to you one last time."

"No," she cried. "I am not a slut to be used and thrown aside. What do you take me for?" Ben flashed into her mind. It ought to have been *him* to jilt her, but a nagging fear filled her. She forced herself to concentrate. How *would* she feel to be thrown over? If Ben gave her up, it would be good. He'd be the big man. Relief was not the emotion she needed to show. Quickly she summoned up how aggrieved she'd been that he'd stopped sending her money. If she hadn't gotten this job, who knew how she would have managed? The last thing she wanted was to depend financially on Joumi. She could not bear to think he might suspect her motives. Too, her anger at the very thought of continuing as any man's kept woman enraged her. Such emotion must have shone through her voice and body.

Ebisu glowered quite convincingly and thrust her against the paneled door where she slipped to the floor, her hand covering her mouth. Somehow she managed to get to her feet, feigning heartbreak, and stretching out her hands to Ebisu. "Don't leave me," she begged, truly acting now, pleased she could so easily take on a false role.

"Get out of my way," the brusque main character said, and Ebisu stepped around her, laughing, managing to give her a sly pat on her rump the cameras couldn't see before he strode through the door.

The director yelled, "Cut."

Shame, remembering how she'd encouraged Ben, made Amaya's face flush.

The director was grinning. "Excellent," he said to her. "That's a take." He turned to the rest of the cast and camera crew. "Boys and girls, enjoy your last evening here. I have paid for your baths and dinner is on me."

After an hour's break, they met at the best hot spring in the village. Fragrant moisture full of the scent of gardenias arose from a deep pool surrounded by ferns and flower gardens. On wooden benches next to the sheer rock face dotted by delicate pine trees several people were lounging with towels draped across their laps or wrapped around their shoulders. Many of the actors were already soaking in the pool.

Amaya couldn't wait. It had been a long time since she'd gotten to enjoy a bath like this one. She rushed into the changing room, stripped off her clothes, and leapt naked into the hot water. Bathing with people who felt like family made her smile happily. The warm water against her bare skin soothed and refreshed. Ebisu looked more handsome than ever. He had a big ego though, but Amaya enjoyed him flirting with her. He splashed her gently and smiled suggestively. Seeing him naked in the water turned her on, she had to admit, but her fantasy was about Joumi. She longed to disrobe in front of him and feel his lean body pressed against hers.

She swam gracefully away from the actor, putting a couple of other girls between him and her, but he didn't give up so easily. After they'd toweled off and gotten dressed, and were walking near a pretty stream that flowed through the center of town, he grabbed her fingers trying to draw her into a pine copse. She laughed at him, snatched her hand away, and skipped after the others. It might make him angry to be rebuffed, and she didn't want to hurt her career by making enemies, but she did not want him, and she would not sell herself again.

At dinner, he grabbed the seat next to hers, but she hardly spoke to him, unable to stop daydreaming about being alone with Joumi. He'd be in Kurakawa tomorrow. The very thought made her weak. As much as she wanted to enjoy the celebration and listen to the excited chatter of the other actors, Joumi filled her mind with dreams she couldn't wait to realize. They were going to Joetsu near the Japan Sea, and then farther north across the mountains to spend a night in Sendai before heading out to Matsushima Bay for two nights. A boat tour of the pretty islands sounded delightful, but a private room where they'd be alone thrilled her more. She felt sure they would consummate their love during this trip. She felt as if she were going on her honeymoon.

Glancing over at Ebisu, she smiled, took her leave, and skipped back to her room, totally unaware of his lascivious gaze upon her back.

~ * ~

Joumi also felt eager to spend time with Amaya away from the troubles of his life. He'd invested all his money in the auto company, and now wondered if he'd made a mistake. Perhaps he ought to have opened a publishing house. They'd sprung up everywhere since the war ended. Yet, many had already folded. He groaned at the thought of losing his money, but he still had three valuable diamonds stashed away in his house. He put aside his worries and smiled calmly as he drove toward the woman he loved. Neither had said another word about England. It was just as well to let the matter drop.

He smiled to himself about the time spent in her flat when he'd continued to be circumspect, bringing her sweets, enjoying a glass of wine or a beer with her, but giving her nothing more physical than a kiss on her cheek. He'd noticed her thrill when he'd brushed his arm against her breast. She'd known it was no accident and had begun to tease him back, occasionally peeking modestly between his legs and raising her eyebrows. He'd laugh so much his penis did not spring to life as she'd hoped. When she intentionally sat close to him on the mat near the dining table, laying her silky thigh against his was a different matter. He had a good mind to begin wearing robes instead of trousers, but the fun and games between them fired both of them with longing.

Just as pleasing were their conversations. He'd thought her naïve and unschooled, but she demonstrated great intelligence and an ability to thwart him intellectually in their debates about whether or not their emerging form of democracy wrongfully defied the old traditions. He'd brought her around to realizing their former government led them into debilitating war. It'd all started in 1931 with their invasion of Manchuria draining their resources. She'd finally agreed the Emperor was a mere figurehead not a god. He'd given wrongful credibility to foolish militaristic talk about how Japan led the way of the people of Asia into freedom.

Amaya'd made him realize in some ways they had a better opportunity with the Americans in power over them. "It's not that I particularly like Americans," she'd declared. "I too want them to leave Japan. We have a proud history, Joumi. For three thousand years our people have been loyal and moral. We must do our best to learn from the Americans now, and win them over, so they can learn from us too. They are very young in their thinking. There is much they need to learn from us, but I am so happy to have more freedom. It has not been easy, but I am in many ways better off now than I could ever have been had we not been defeated. At least now we are allowed to think for ourselves. Women even get to vote."

"All is splendid," he'd responded. "Provided it goes along with MacArthur's plans for us."

"True." Amaya glanced sideways at him with a cheeky smile playing around her lips. "What plans do you have for me, my love? Anything special?"

~ * ~

As he pulled his car off the main highway onto a narrow cobbled street of the village, her words and suggestive looks bounced around in his mind. He could almost smell the sweetness of her perfume.

He drove slowly, defying his desire to rush. This village was exquisite. No wonder they'd wanted to film in this place. Hemmed in by pine trees and mountains, with sparkling streams gurgling under little wooden bridges, flashing across stones, it exuded harmony. One hot spring had a pretty thatched portico to shade bathers. It would give peace to many people to see some of the old beauty of traditional Japanese life, he thought. He considered suggesting they stay here.

On a narrow sidewalk outside the inn where the actors had been housed, he saw Amaya waiting for him. She raised her hand to wave. Her slender figure in a golden kimono made his palms sweaty. He wanted to shout joyously at the top of his lungs. Such a heated response made him smile at the emotion she managed to stir in him. He intentionally slowed down. By nature he was quiet and thoughtful.

Before he stopped his car, a man strode out behind her and grabbed her around her waist, spun her around, and kissed her soundly on her mouth.

Joumi hit the accelerator and sped past them right through the village up a mountain path, which turned into a dirt road and forced him to stop. His mind raced with accusations. "How could she," he raged, thumping the dashboard so hard, it bruised his knuckle. He climbed out of the car and leaned against the bonnet, staring down into the woods at a pristine stream trickling across rocks into a deep pool. He smelled the woodsy air and finally calmed down enough to realize it was not *she* who'd initiated the kissing. In fact, hadn't the man accosted *her*? With this thought, his anger shifted to the man who most surely was one of her fellow actors.

Joumi'd said he wanted her to fulfill her dreams and he did, but if she was to be his wife, perhaps it would be best for her to give up her acting career. He'd been planning to ask her to marry him, but now he was not so sure. Perhaps, he needed to find out who *was* this man taking advantage of a young woman in such an outrageous manner in public, unless he'd intentionally wanted to scare Joumi off. Had he seen Joumi driving up? Had Amaya told him about them? Joumi's thoughts refused to settle down. For a long time he stared into space trying to decide what to do next.

~ * ~

"Joumi." The velvet straps of Amaya's getas cut into her toes. Probably she had blisters. Now she wished she owned more practical shoes to wear rather than these pretty wooden sandals that matched her kimono. She hadn't expected to have to walk a mile but it was a relief to see the car with Joumi leaning dejectedly against the front tire. She'd seen his car motoring toward her and her heart had soared. She'd raised her hand in greeting to him, smiling broadly, but without warning she'd been grabbed, spun around and kissed. When Joumi did not stop but continued driving past her, she'd been outraged. She turned to Ebisu. "You pig!" She'd slapped him hard across his face, leaving a red welt.

"Joumi," she repeated again softly. He did not turn around but she knew he'd heard her. She'd seen his head turn slightly in her direction. "Won't you look at me? Please." How exasperating his jealousy could be. He had nothing to be jealous about. She wanted to tell him to stop being a fool spoiling their time together, which she knew he'd wanted as much as she. But perhaps he hadn't. Perhaps seeing Ebisu gave him the excuse he needed to forgo her. *I am being silly*, she thought, realizing she was confusing her actress role with reality.

"Why didn't you stop?" She slipped out of her sandals and, trying not to wince, tiptoed across the pebbles and sticks to his side. She touched his back, but still he resisted turning around and facing her imploring eyes. "Please," she begged. "At least look at me."

Joumi began shaking from both rage and spent emotion. Part of him wanted to beg her to forgive his behavior, but part of him doubted her and wanted to punish her. *Let her suffer awhile,* he cruelly thought, intentionally ignoring the soft feel of her gentle hand upon his shoulder, not allowing himself to be soothed by the fragrance of her flowery perfume. He would not let himself be fooled.

At last, with a deep sigh, she moved away. "I will not beg you," she said. "I am going back to Tokyo."

"You've missed the last bus," he growled, at last managing to speak.

"Then I will walk," she countered, and began limping away, retrieving her sandals but not attempting to put them on. She knew *he* was being ridiculous and stubborn. But she could play that game too. Already feeling weak from hiking so far in her ill-equipped sandals, she had no idea how she'd ever be able to make it much farther. She'd been too excited three weeks ago to pay attention to how far it actually was on the bus from the station to Kurokawa. What did it matter? She'd be lucky to stumble back to the village, let alone onto the station by foot. She certainly would not be able to carry all her luggage.

Watching her hobble along obviously in pain broke through Joumi's resistance. He couldn't bear to see her hurt. "Amaya," he cried, chasing after her, and falling to his knees at her feet. He raised one small foot, tenderly examining the red marks. He kissed her toes. "You must be sore." He stood and took her hand. "Come," he commanded gently.

Amaya obediently hobbled after him, half-leaning upon him, wondering why he was leading her into the trees. Did he intend for their love-making to begin here? She did not want it so, although it was a pretty place.

Not far from the road, they came to little waterfall gurgling over some smooth rocks. Joumi sat her on a big stone and gently put her feet into the cool running water. "There," he said, standing behind her, his fingers massaging her shoulders. "We shall not speak of what happened," he said.

Amaya liked his hands upon her shoulders, and the cold water chilled her bruised feet, but his words chilled her. She wanted to cry, *speak of what?* She was afraid because in her heart she did not think Ebisu's unwelcome kiss was the problem. It was a trigger to the bigger lie between them. How desperately she wanted to tell Joumi she'd never loved Ben Britton, and she'd written to him to call things off forever. How could she when Joumi preferred denial over truth? For the first time, although she'd dreamed of becoming his wife, she wondered if perhaps they'd be better off apart.

Seven

Joumi and Amaya sat silently side by side on the drive back to Tokyo. They'd decided to postpone their trip. Joumi stared at the road doing his best to ignore how despondent he felt. He was poignantly aware of how careful they were both being not to touch shoulders like they usually did. The wide comfortable seat of his car never seemed so lonely and unwelcome. Luxury separated and did not comfort them.

Amaya stared into the horizon too, paying little attention to what they passed, sad for not being able to appreciate the beauty of the trees and the high rocky hills. She glanced sideways at Joumi. His hand rigidly clutched the steering wheel. Amaya refused to show how hurt she felt. After Joumi'd declared their trip would not be a good time for them and then mumbled he hadn't realized he had business he needed to attend at home, she'd smiled agreeably, patted his hand as if he were a child. He was. It was a feeble excuse. He knew it.

She'd recently read in a new woman's magazine what women deserved in relationships. Tenderness and heat. She'd thought Joumi her ideal. How could she have been so mistaken? This stubborn man's playing hard to get no longer seemed titillating. She wanted a real man. Her thoughts slipped to Ebisu, but she quickly dismissed such a ridiculous idea. He certainly did not want commitment and was probably married. They'd never had a normal conversation so she had no idea of his marital status.

Her ire increased to remember her dead husband's infidelities. She, like all women, was supposed to accept men chasing other girls as if it were an acceptable norm. What rubbish, she thought, using one of Ben's sayings. Why should any woman have to endure kowtowing to her unfaithful husband, preparing his dinner, bringing his slippers, and all the while being pretty and accessible?

Once again she glanced over at Joumi, aware of his strong chin, his wiry arms, his kindness, and she wanted to hate him, but she couldn't. "You are a fool," she cried. "I have done nothing wrong. What do you think? That I invited Ebisu's advances? It was a game to him, nothing but a silly game. He wants an easy fuck like all you men." She *almost* begged him to turn the car around and drive to Joetsu as they'd planned, but pride and anger buried her words deep in her throat as if she might strangle. He was the one who needed to atone, not *she.*

Joumi grunted. He knew he'd overreacted but he couldn't help himself. Amaya was everything to him, his hope for love, his longing for a future, his dreams for a family. Yet he could not put out of his mind that perhaps her very impurity invited flirtations from men. After a long pause of perhaps five miles of driving, he spoke. "I am not a game-player. I am not interested in easy women."

"I am not one," Amaya cried.

They drove another thirty miles in stony silence. He at least was stony, but she was storming, hating him to look down upon her when she had done nothing but survive. The Englishman who she no longer wished to even call by name had never been anything more to her than economic necessity. Why should women always bear the brunt of blame for sexual infidelity? What about men who thought nothing of forgetting their wives and children?

Her mind turned back to when she'd been a young girl transplanted away from her dear mother and her family into her husband's life. He'd often come home drunk smelling of other women's scents, and yet expected her to have dinner ready, a hot bath prepared, her body oiled. How dare he! How dare any man treat her this way! Never again. In an act of defiance, she began to sing a popular tune in English, "Come, come, everybody. Let's all sing a happy song."

Joumi froze. Her soldier-man no doubt taught her to speak *his* language. Joumi knew he was being unfair. This song was used to cheer people up and help them learn the language of their conquerors. Plus everyone had the Japanese/English translation, *Nichi-Bei Kaiwa Techō*. Nevertheless, he was speechless because he'd suddenly realized perhaps she *could* speak English and that was another secret she hadn't shared with him.

When Joumi continued to sit in icy silence, she'd had more than enough. "Pull over," she cried. "I would rather walk than endure your cold treatment of me when I have done no wrong. I was so looking forward to our trip and you have spoiled everything."

Joumi reached his hand across and took hers. "I am sorry," was all he said.

She refused to shed one tear, but necessity kept her quiet and she remained seated. Even though she'd begun to recognize her surroundings, it would be hell to walk the remaining distance home. They still had five miles to go before they got to her apartment complex.

Neither said a word to the other as they finished the journey to Amaya's flat.

"I *am* sorry," Joumi repeated as she got out of the car. He sat with his head almost on the dashboard while she angrily gathered her bags and dragged them to the door of the building. He knew he ought to help her but he felt like a slug, as defeated as they'd all once been. *I must make a joke,* he thought, *to soften this anger*. Words would not come. At last, he chased her into the building and seized her biggest suitcase, heaving it into the elevator.

"I don't need your help," she stated forlornly.

"Very well." He stepped away from the closing door. "I won't bother you again. Goodbye."

~ * ~

That night Amaya cried herself to sleep but in the morning she'd recovered. She had a good mind to contact Ebisu but knew she was merely being an opportunist. She refused to get in touch with Joumi even though she knew he had a telephone. He'd given her his number insisting she could call him about anything.

Anything! Huh! If her heart had not been turned toward love, she'd certainly have poisoned him.

Hours and days went by, before she was to resume filming, with no sign of Joumi. Why didn't he come here and make everything right between them! He was too obstinate. Still, she hoped, yearned, and wished, not venturing out except to buy a few groceries, always hurrying home. She thought she ought to leave a note on her door. What if he'd come and she'd been gone? Would he wait? Would he try again? Every footstep in the corridor made her eyes open wide with hope and expectation, but when the steps went past her door, she felt herself, body and soul, droop. It was all she could manage to eat rice cakes.

At last, with only one more day before she went to Kyoto, she got up her courage, left a note on her door and went out, heading for what was left of a Shinto shrine not far away. The hole in the arched roof let in sunlight. It warmed the top of her head but made her feel even more worthless. The iron Amida sculpture that used to sit on a raised platform under the pagoda roof had been stolen, perhaps turned into pots and pans. Looking up at the sky, she raised her arms, "Please," she whispered, "Amida. Give me peace. Bring Joumi back to me. Please, Amida." Tears flooded her eyes. "Forgive me. I have done bad things. How can I ever enter the Pure Land?"

Amaya remembered the words of Honen Shonin. The monk said all that was necessary to get into heaven and be reunited with loved ones, and hear their fond chatter, and smell divine fragrances, and bathe in blissful waters full of lotus blossoms was to recite Amida's name with a contrite heart. "Amida, Amida," she tried repeating, but felt no peace. Her anguish, if anything, seemed worse. Calling out a holy name only belonged to good people, not people like her who did not feel contrite and never would. She had survived and who could blame her for preferring to be the concubine of one man rather than a slut to many?

Amaya returned to her flat. The note fluttered in a breeze. Clearly she had not missed his visit. He had not bothered to come. Her mind made up, if he did not show up within the hour and apologize before she left, she would never see him again.

She began repacking her bags with the belongings she'd pulled out and left scattered on the floor. Many of her kimonos lay crumpled on top of wrinkled slacks, skirts and blouses. She did not bother with the sandals she'd worn in her pursuit of Joumi, but packed several other pairs of pretty shoes. Her toes still hurt, reminding her of how foolish she must have seemed, how desperate, how easy. The wooden clogs, coated with mud, were a harsh reminder. She decided she would wash them later and sell them. Money was dwindling and she couldn't afford another pair but what did it matter? If her next and last scene in the movie went well, the director might take her on permanently. She'd get a regular salary, small, but enough to keep her going.

When she heard the elevator door squeak open, she paused, holding up the lacy lingerie she'd bought to wear for Joumi. About to put it into a cloth bag, she waited, her heart thumping in her chest, as heavy footsteps boomed along the walkway. They stopped in front of her door. She dropped the underwear, rushed to her mirror, quickly tucking a strand of stray black hair behind her ear, smoothing her face with powder, smearing on lipstick, and then wiping it off. Joumi did not want a pan pan.

For some reason the distinct rap on the door chilled her, but she told herself it was natural to be anxious after their argument, which was so much more than a mere row. It seemed an unbearable abyss. She thought she could stand anything if only Joumi had brought her sweets and they could share tea together.

The rap sounded again. More loudly. More insistent.

She peered through the glass door panels at the shadowy outline of a man. It was not Joumi. Who could it be? Taken aback, she slid the door open.

A tall, elegant man in a white suit smiled and took off his panama hat. She wanted to be wrong, but she could not mistake the too familiar face so full of lust. It was Ben Briton.

"Amaya, my love." He dropped his leather case on the concrete walkway, and reached for her, crushing her against his chest so she could hardly breathe.

Her thoughts raged. What was he doing here? How dare he ignore her letter? But maybe it would be for the best. No never. Hadn't she promised Amida? "No," she shouted. "You had no business coming here. Didn't you get my letter?"

"Hush," he said, stroking her hair as if she were a little girl. "I got your note, but I knew you were only trying to spare Lucy and the children. I knew you'd feel better once we got together." He released his hold on her and stepped back. "You are as beautiful as ever. More so."

Amaya stared into his admiring eyes, sickened as much by her past behavior as by this man who seemed to her a stranger. "You should not have come, but since you are here, come in and I will make us tea." She needed time to plan her strategy. Her thoughts turned to the money he hadn't sent. Remorse flooded her with repulsion for him and for herself. She turned her back on him and fled into her flat, wishing she could shut him out, but knowing she'd have to sweet-talk him somehow to let him down easily.

She couldn't bear to betray herself even with words.

She went back and faced him, putting a stern look on her face, trying to be like a stately elder woman such as her grandmother had been, someone too formidable to ignore. "Ben," she said with a catch of fear in her throat. "After tea, you must go home. You do not belong here."

He tossed his hat onto the sofa, and eyed her for a moment. "What do you mean I don't belong? I'm the one paid for this." He waved his arm around the room and wrapped it around her shoulders forcing a kiss upon her, his tongue almost in the back of her throat, making her choke.

She managed to squirm away, nauseated. "Please stop." Now she remembered how horrible he'd been before, worse even than her husband, coming into her flat as if he owned her, forcing his wishes upon her with no foreplay to make things pleasant.

"You can't deny me now." He gripped her arms and stared at her, his face full of excitement. "I've traveled a long way for this moment."

She knew she had some blame for sending him titillating letters, telling him stupid lies about his prowess, his strength, the size of his cock, but she was done with such a life, such a need, such slavery. "Let go of me," she demanded. "I told you. I don't love you. I only wrote those things so you'd give me money and pay the rent. I no longer need you. Please go away."

His hands tightened around her arms, his fingers digging into her flesh. He looked confused, dazed. He shook his head slightly as if he did not understand her, but she'd spoken English.

"You must leave," she cried. "Immediately. My boyfriend will be here any minute and he will kill you. He is a gangster and very dangerous."

"Boyfriend? You have been unfaithful all this time?" He looked as if he might cry.

"Oh Ben, you don't want me. I am only a dream to you. A hope for something unreal. I am sorry I led you on. You must have tea and then leave. We will be friends. It's the only way."

"I've bought you a visa to return with me to England," he said, now watching her with a look of ruthless power, the look of a conqueror who always had his way. "You will return with me and be my wife. As agreed."

"I never agreed. You don't own me." she cried, trying to shake off his hold on her arms.

"Then why did you accept my money?" His voice shook with fury.

Amaya tried to find a way to turn the storm on his face and his gritted teeth into peace. "You helped me so much, Ben," she moaned softly, remembering the Americans said to tell the truth. "I am in love with another man. His name is Joumi. Besides, you stopped sending money months ago. You know that. I was sure you'd forgotten about me."

"I had not forgotten." His eyes looked even more stormy. He threw her onto the couch and, holding her down with one hand around her throat, tugged his hat out from under her shoulders, and sliced it through the air so that it landed on the low slung table in the other room.

"Let me go," she cried, trying to pull his hand away from her neck. "What are you doing?"

He stared down at her. "You'd better pretend just like you always did." He ripped her kimono away and put his mouth on her breast sucking so painfully, she cried out. He took his fist and punched her hard. If her head had not been against a pillow, he would have snapped her neck.

"Bitch," he shouted, unbuttoning his trousers. "Pretend you are a bitch in heat."

He lumbered on top of her pinning her down, pulling up her kimono and ripping her panties to one side.

She struggled but was helpless to get out from under his bulk.

As he thrust his penis into her, she cried out again and again, but he would not stop. Her powerlessness and her pain seemed to make him even more excited. At last with a groan of pleasure he ejaculated. As he continued to flop on top of her, she wanted to impale herself on a knife, but the longer he lay grunting above her, the calmer she became. She would not murder herself, but *him*. He began to snore, his breathing heavy. Smelling whisky fumes, she realized he'd been boozing. She managed to heave him to one side, leaving him on the couch. Her vagina felt bruised and torn.

From her kitchen she fetched a fish knife and stood above him thinking she would cut his throat and stab him through his heart. He'd been many things in the past, cold, rough, hungry for love, but never a rapist. Blood dripped down her leg pooling on the floor next to the couch. His snores got louder, more guttural, more disgusting, but she couldn't do it. She couldn't kill, not him, not anyone.

She turned away. Every step made her want to cry at the sting of pain both physical and emotional. She got herself into the bathroom, dropped the knife, and bathed herself, wincing at the cold water. She picked up and wadded the white lacy panties and used them as a pad, hurrying to dress in baggy trousers. She threw on a bright red shirt. She could not remain here. He might wake up and rape her again.

It seemed to take forever but was only a minute or so before she'd picked up her cloth bag, the one with her makeup and a few necessaries, and crept from her apartment, leaving the door open. Her body ached from head to toe, but her heart ached more. Where could she go? Who would want her now? Even Ginza Girl seemed too far away. She couldn't face a trolley ride. Her head hanging, she dragged herself, going anywhere, anywhere away from this atrocity.

~ * ~

Joumi watched the dejected back of a woman wearing a red shirt hobbling away. For a moment he thought it might be Amaya, but this woman looked frail and troubled. He dismissed such a dejected figure as just one more starving female who'd not got a pot for cooking rice and no one to cook for. In his hand he held a plate of Amaya's favorite noodle dish with octopus.

For several days, he'd fumed more at himself than at her, wanting to go to her house, but then, called away, this time truly on business about the Flying Feathers, he had been unable to visit her and apologize. What a fool he'd been. He wanted to kick himself, kill himself, and find some way to atone, but in the end, there was little he could do except throw himself on her mercy. So here he was carrying a gift to make amends, a meal he knew she loved. Would she, he wondered, accept him back?

As he made his way out of the elevator onto her floor, he rehearsed his words. *Please,* he begged in his mind, *give me another chance. I know I made a stupid mistake. I deserve for you to tell me to go away forever. I love you.* This was her last day in Tokyo before going off to Kyoto. He felt embarrassed at his absurd reaction to that stupid actor, Ebizu, but he didn't entirely blame himself. The man *was* handsome, confident and wealthy. Joumi *was* jealous and insecure. His passion was burning a hole in his heart and in his life, but he did not want to live without Amaya. He only hoped she still felt the same way. He once again rehearsed his words as he approached her door. *I am sorry. Forgive me. I want you to marry me.*

The door was open. How strange.

Eight

Amaya's face throbbed with pain. She knew she must look a sight, but she didn't care. She had to get away from *him*. She went directly to the station and found a toilet with a mirror. One eye was black and blue and her mouth was swollen and red from where he'd forced his mouth upon hers. How could she go to Kyoto tomorrow looking like this? Even heavy makeup would not hide her bruises. She would be dismissed from her role. Her acting career would be over. If she didn't show up, it would be the same. They'd blacklist her.

Who could she go to for help? Not Joumi. She couldn't face him. How would she explain? Unless she lied and said the rape had been random, or simply that she'd been beaten but not mention the rape. She could say she'd been robbed. But Joumi'd already made it clear he wanted nothing more to do with her. Her weak spirits sank. She leaned against the sink aware of the dank odor of dirty drains. An older woman walked by her and quickly looked away. It crossed her mind to try to find her dead husband's mother, but they'd never gotten along.

She needed support but who would help her? Ginza Girl might be her only hope, yet Amaya was reluctant to call on her again. Girl knew about Joumi and would almost certainly insist Amaya contact him. A tiny hope flared and quickly died. If Amaya went to Girl's even to stay for a few nights until her face looked better, she'd have to listen to moans from sex acts. Amaya hadn't until this moment realized how superior she'd felt over girls of the night, even Girl. She hung her head. She was no better than any other pan pan, but she'd wanted to escape sexual slavery by becoming a paid actress, and thought she might have a chance. Now things seemed bleak.

Even her latest role deflated her when she considered she played a young girl seduced by a hateful man who'd wanted nothing more than to satisfy his lust. The notion of seduction of young girls who were then cast aside did not deserve to be applauded. In fact, at this moment she despised the whole idea of the movie.

Another woman in a smart business suit stood behind Amaya. "Excuse me," she said sounding none too polite. "Are you done yet?"

"There's no soap," Amaya said, stepping away from the sink.

The woman's face in the cloudy mirror reminded Amaya of Ebisu. Perhaps it was her self-satisfied look as she briskly rinsed her hands. Who knew what that look was about? Surely, it had nothing to do with her asking Amaya to get out of the way? Who could understand what lay in the hearts and minds of people? Who could fathom what caused any of them to act the way they did? Amaya's mind shied away from Ben Briton. *Him*, she didn't want to think about ever again. She turned her thoughts to Ebisu, latching onto his image as if he were her savior.

Maybe Ebisu's flirtatiousness had been precipitated by the nature of the movie and his role in it, she thought. Maybe actors could not separate the roles they played with their everyday identity. Ebisu might be a decent guy but he'd become the overbearing Japanese man he'd portrayed in the movie. For some reason, in spite of this insight, Amaya did not want Ebisu to come to her rescue. She wanted him to like her as a person and not see her as a victim. Not that she cared about him. It wasn't *that*. Of course, he might be influential in helping her develop a career. He might even be sympathetic to what had happened. What if he expected sexual favors?

Amaya groaned. The woman in the smart suit dried her hands and left, making room for two more women to come into the confining bathroom. They were waiting outside the stalls. Her eyes met the closest lady's, who muttered something to her friend. They quickly walked out of the lavatory intentionally avoiding Amaya's presence. How was it that in a city of millions, she had no one?

~ * ~

Joumi stared into the empty apartment. The first thing he noticed was a pool of blood next to the couch. What happened here? "Amaya," he called, his voice alarmed. He stepped into the room and only then did he see the man slumped on the couch. Joumi recoiled. What was this? No, he must not allow his jealousy to get the better of him. "Amaya, where are you?" he shouted. The man on the sofa grunted and turned over onto his back, not waking.

Joumi rushed into the dining room. She was not there, but her large suitcase lay open near the screen that hid her sleeping mat. So she must not have gone to Kyoto yet. In the bathroom, he found her ripped kimono heaped on the floor. He knew then. He knew who the man was and what he'd done. The horror he now faced within was not jealousy but a rage he had not known he possessed. It consumed all attempts at being rational.

He stormed into the sitting room and hit the man in his face instantly reviving the guy who tried to get to his feet to defend himself. Joumi kicked his shin, aware the man's flaccid dick was hanging out of his opened trousers. He had no words to express his contempt, his disgust, his desire to put an end to this bully's life forever. He made a fist, preparing to strike again, but the man moaned, his hands moving rapidly from his groin to his chest. He gasped. "Help me," he begged. "I need a doctor."

Joumi watched him gasping for breath, heard his cries of agony until, blue in the face with neck muscles like ropes, he slumped forward unconscious.

Joumi wished he had more than a fist, perhaps a wooden board from the river, or a metal plate from a bomb, or anything solid, defiant, ugly and strong to crash into the man's skull, silencing him forever, preventing him from ever again forcing himself on innocent women. *Amaya,* he cried in his mind. *My sweet Amaya.* He stepped away from Briton, not wanting even a hem of his clothing to touch this brute. *Aah,* Joumi cried inside, looking around for a weapon, seeing only a teapot, *her* teapot.

He needed to do nothing.

The Englishman made a gurgling noise and a rattle shook his chest. It took perhaps five seconds and the man was dead.

It was no relief that this violator was lifeless. None at all. *Chikushou. Damn, damn, damn,* the expletives leaped from Joumi's mouth. The Englishman might be the perpetrator of evil against Amaya, especially in this his final act of 'love,' but he represented the tangle of lives, of wars, of peace, of people's heartless obedience to ruthless rulers. *Why did we not rise against our militarist government years ago,* Joumi lamented? *Why did we not stop what happened?* He did not care about Americans dying or English soldiers skewered upon bayonets, but he knew it all to be a part of an ugly story of humankind. He knew, too, he was impotent to stop it, to stop any of it, and he himself had contributed to such hate, such greed, all in the name of survival, but it was more than that. For him it had been a matter of power too. Why had he not taken Amaya away when he'd had the chance?

Joumi stared at the dead man. He did not care about *his* family if he had one, but he sorrowed for Amaya who'd not only been his victim. She'd used him for her purposes too. She'd played the guy. Joumi knew from his sources that Briton continued to send money but it had been stolen, leaving Amaya more and more financially helpless. He, the great Joumi, had planned to step in to save her. Now he recognized his desire to help her for what it was—an attempt to control her and force her to love him. He felt singularly undesirable, and always had, even before he became a man of means.

"Where is she? What have you done?" Joumi cried ineffectually. "Amaya, Amaya, my love." He sank onto his haunches with his hands over his face and began to groan. This hated rival would never again open his cool blue eyes. Joumi was glad, but now what to do with the body?

~ * ~

Amaya marveled at her ability to keep on living. It seemed as if all her normal bodily functions ought to have shut down, but in spite of having been violated, she needed to pee, badly. She didn't want to be in this smelly station toilet with other women listening to her urinate. They made her feel ashamed and guilty for *what* she could not discern. She had done nothing! She had resisted.

Her feet dragged her outside. She found a small bamboo patch where she dropped her trousers and peed. Her white lace panties were stained with blood, but the worst bleeding was over. She wiped herself with the stained lingerie and left it in the bamboo before standing up. There was nothing but to trudge forward. Where, where, she wondered, as she began limping about the streets of Tokyo. So many places, so many people, so many hovels, so many stands springing up, and nowhere for her to rest.

At last, she came by the Kabuki Theater, regretting at how she'd rebuffed Joumi who'd wanted to bring her here. The next show was not until later, but when she tried the door, it opened and she stepped inside, hurrying past the ticket office. No one stopped her. She sat on a bench to the rear of the stage and stared at the cherry tree painted on the drop curtain behind the platform. In front of this backdrop the actors, all male, would dance, sing, and impersonate women playing the shamisen. They would make people laugh and cry. It's what she wanted to do! She almost began weeping, but could not.

With no backrest on the wooden bench, she lay prone, expecting to be discovered and expelled from this entertainment palace with its dragon decorations and glowing lamps. She didn't much care. Sleep, perhaps as an antidote for her utter exhaustion, overtook her, and she closed her eyes. If she had been able, she would surely have recited the name of Amida. Yet she dreamed of shining streets weaving through a tropical garden full of lotus ponds. She thought she heard her mother's voice. It made her smile, and her sore mouth did not hurt much, but enough to rouse her. At first she did not know where she was, who she was, and she didn't remember what had happened. Soon enough her agony returned. She cried out upon awakening and sat up straight, wishing she were dead.

"Hey, Lady," a voice to the left of where she sat spoke. "You awake now?"

She nodded, holding her breath, but managed. "Don't worry, I'll leave..."

"Stay," the voice which she thought could be either male or female responded.

Amaya wondered *could this be one of the troupe? A man who acted as a woman?* In spite of her upset, she felt intrigue. "Who are you?" she asked. "Do you work here?"

"I do, but not what you think. I take care of the wigs and costumes. You want to be my assistant, hanii?"

Amaya stared at the figure shrouded in the darkness lit only by a couple of lanterns. The face was that of a woman, but she couldn't be sure. She was afraid to ask. "Would you pay me? Where would I stay?"

A deep chuckle sounded. "You stay with me. I live above the theater."

"What do you want from me?" Amaya was alarmed.

"I will teach you how to comb the hair and sew new wigs. You will learn how to paint faces kumadori style. Can you hold a brush steady? Do you know how to apply face powder? Are you willing to help actors with their robes? Are you able to keep your mouth shut?"

Amaya hung her head. "I don't know," she muttered. "How much will you pay me? I will not have sex with you."

"What makes you think I'd fancy you?" the voice laughed again, deep, filled with humor. "I will teach you what you need to know. Come along, young lady. I think you have been hurt. I will help you."

Amaya could not help but trust this person. Since she had nowhere to go, she accepted the hand, a leathery claw that had known much manual labor, offered to her When she stood up and stepped into the passage off to one side, she discovered slight as she, Amaya, was and small in stature, she towered over the person offering her help. A dwarf. Her eyes, filling with pity, sought her rescuer's eyes.

"Ah, now you know. We are both outcasts. My hands do not serve me well these days. You need not fear me. You have been sent to me because I must have a helper, or I will be on the street."

Amaya managed a tiny bow, taking in the tiny but colorful kimono worn by this little person, this lady. "Thank you," she uttered. "I was so tired. I did not know where to go."

"Come, follow me. I live in the attic. It is quite large and I have made it comfortable."

~ * ~

Joumi's anger sagged. He'd arrived not knowing what to expect from Amaya, but now he wanted to burn this cold flat down. It had been warm before with her life, but with this corpse contaminating the sitting room, it seemed to Joumi it must always have been tainted by a hateful presence. He stared at the unmoving silent remains. The soul had no doubt fled, but where might such a one go after such evil. Joumi wished him born again in the body of a river rat.

Where had Amaya fled? *I must find her,* he thought, and strode out the door, carefully sliding it shut to conceal what lay within. He would deal with the body later. He had no intention of calling the police or the hospital. Neither could help and scandal might harm Amaya even further.

On the street, he stood looking in both

directions. Which way had she gone? Suddenly he realized that pathetic woman he'd seen limping away had been *her*. His shoulders seemed to cave in upon himself, but he had no time to regret he'd not recognized her. She'd been going in the direction of the station. Certainly, if he were she, he'd go there and get on the first train out of the place that caused so much misery. He knew she must be wretched and he did not want her to spend one further moment without his protective arms around her to comfort her, hold her, and reassure her.

At the station, he looked everywhere, even going into the restrooms. He stopped strangers to ask them if they'd seen a woman wearing a bright red shirt. Some looked away, others merely shook their heads and moved off, one old lady said *iie* with a sorrowful look. Before she could elaborate, perhaps with a shocking story about her losses, he bowed graciously, and hurried out of the station. He did not know which way to go, but decided to try the bank where he knew she'd exchanged pounds for yen.

The bank building had suffered a little damage but had been immaculately restored, its banner freshly painted, its revolving doors well-oiled. In the lobby, Joumi searched the faces of the cashiers, looking for the boy one of his minions had paid for information. When his eyes rested upon the lad who knew about Amaya, he was busy counting money. He seemed to feel Joumi's look and glanced up. Upon seeing Joumi, he turned pale, perhaps realizing who he was. The clerk quickly put the money into his cash drawer and shut the window.

Joumi wasted no time. In a few strides he stood in front of him and tapped on the closed pane. "Open up," he demanded. "Have you seen Amaya?"

The boy looked frightened and slid the window open only a few inches. "Not for months," he responded.

Joumi had no time to reassure the kid he wasn't going to report him for revealing privileged client information. He realized searching for Amaya on foot was hopeless. Dejected, he walked back to her apartment building, where he'd left his car, and got in and drove down the street.

Joumi parked in the Ginza district and went in search of flunkies from the Ueda gang who he'd known in the past. He did not like dealing with such underworld thugs. He'd long ago distanced himself from gangs. He wasn't sure he could trust them to not get caught or to try to blackmail him later, but having the corpse completely disappear seemed the best way out for all of them. It took no time for him to find them. After exchanging money with a promise for more, he quickly left. They were to provide him with proof they'd disposed of the body.

Hopefully not many knew Briton was here in Tokyo. No one here would miss him and no one would care what sort of burial he got. This pervert did not deserve a decent send-off. No cigarettes or sweets and certainly no coins would be in any coffin to help him cross the river. Not that Joumi believed in these Buddhist traditions, and yet he understood such ceremony could bring comfort to the relatives of the deceased. Let Briton's family, if he had one back in England, suffer too. As for Briton, the Ueda thugs could toss him in the river, burn his remains in a furnace, or hack it to pieces and feed it to vermin, for all he cared.

Nine

Amaya followed the dwarf behind the stage and through a narrow door. They went upstairs and emerged into an attic full of stage props leaning against the wooden walls, costumes hanging on racks, and various other theater paraphernalia scattered about in disarray. Amaya felt dismayed at the thought of living here, but it would be better than being on the street.

The dwarf led her to the far end of the room and took her behind a screen.

What a difference. Light streamed through a skylight cut into the sloping roof and poured into a clean, luxurious room. It looked more Japanese than Amaya's flat which surprised her because she'd realized the woman who was helping her was a third world person, a Korean. "This is beautiful," she said, her voice full of admiration.

"Junko," the dwarf said. "My friends call me Junko. What is your name?"

"Amaya." Amaya smiled. "Junko is a pretty name." She wanted to ask how come this woman had a Japanese name when she was clearly not native born. The question hung in her mind but she said nothing, not wanting to embarrass her hostess who might be sensitive about being an immigrant.

"Make yourself comfortable," Junko said with a shrewd smile, eying Amaya with a friendly look. "I will prepare some tea. I want to hear all about you."

After the tea was brewed and poured into delicate cups, the two women sat near the brazier. Amaya nursed hers, holding the cup in her hands, glad of the warmth from the glowing charcoal, trying to decide what to tell Junko who had once again asked her about herself. At last her story burst from her. She left nothing out. She spoke softly, looking down at the tiled floor, about her family, and of how she'd been married but was free now and had become an actress. When she mentioned Joumi, her heart sank. She looked up into Junko's kind face. "I am a fraud," she said slowly. "I am not really an actress although I have had a few parts. It is only my dream to be famous."

"And perhaps," Junko interrupted. "To be loved by Joumi?"

"He doesn't want me!" Amaya cried. "He never will now!" She told Junko about Ben Briton and how he had raped her and even now was in her flat so she could never go back there.

Junko listened intently, nodding. "Life is very difficult sometimes, but I am living example of how it can go from bad to better. I was on the streets after my parents died in war, but now am wig-maker, and live in nice place, with regular pay, and Kabuki friends who rely upon me for their costumes, their makeup, and my advice too."

"You must be very wise."

"Nei. Just lucky. You will be lucky again too. You see."

~ * ~

The very next day Joumi drove to Kyoto in the hope Amaya had gone there. It was a long tedious drive taking him eight hours but at least the city had not suffered much damage. Once the capital of Japan, Kyoto had many shrines and holy places. He remembered Amaya saying the filming was to be at a golden temple and went to Kinkaku known for its real gold-leaf walls and exquisite gardens. Sure enough he discovered a film crew busily taking shots of Ebisu and a girl who looked a lot like Amaya. He found the director and asked him if Amaya had arrived yet.

"Amaya has not. She is too late, so far as I'm concerned. This girl is not as good as her and we have to reshoot the earlier scenes. Amaya will never work for me again."

"Perhaps," Joumi said haughtily, "something detained her, something she couldn't help." With that he turned his back, climbed into his car and drove straight to his flat in Tokyo. Although the drive tired him, he made several phone calls to contacts and asked them to try to find Amaya. She must be somewhere in Tokyo he surmised and hoped. Finally, exhausted both emotionally and physically, he laid out his sleeping mat and fell into an uneasy slumber.

First thing in the morning when he awoke, without even drinking tea and eating a rice cake, he set out. After making sure Briton's body was gone and her apartment had been cleaned, and also hoping she might be there, but wasn't, he drove the streets nearby hoping she might appear. She did not.

~ * ~

The days turned into weeks and months. Amaya hoped she could stay hidden the rest of her life. Alas something new happened, something she'd dreaded, and still hoped was not so. She missed two periods. The first one she'd told herself was probably a result of stress, but the second one began to make it obvious. She was famished all the time, and bloated like never before, and beginning to feel nauseous.

Amaya sewed long human hairs that had been bleached white, one by one, onto a headpiece. It was to be a special wig for one of the kabuki actors. He was a slight young man and very handsome but also clearly not interested in women. They'd become friendly perhaps because he did not seem threatening. He was always hungry and she was glad to be able to feed him from Junko's never-ending supply of delicacies that included fish and rice in abundance. She wished he might be her brother and wistfully thought of him as Haruo.

As she sewed hair after hair into place, she felt satisfaction to see the wig becoming fuller. Somehow this mundane and monotonous activity calmed her. Nothing had induced her to go outside and she was grateful to the dwarf for her kindness and friendship. "Junko," she said when her benefactor came into the sitting area. "I am pregnant." Amaya did not know how Junko would respond and was a little frightened. What if she threw her out?

Junko threw her arms in the air in a gesture of delight. "A baby," she screamed. "That is wonderful." Then she hesitated and eyed Amaya carefully. "How are you feeling?"

Amaya didn't have the heart to tell her friend she did not want this child and in fact the very thought of *his* half-breed made her want to kill herself. She couldn't tell Junko. "A baby is a blessing," she muttered, and thought to herself, *but not this one, and not for me.*

Amaya's belly got bigger and bigger. She could feel the life within kicking but it did not please her. It reminded her of how horribly this child had been conceived. Junko loved to lay her ear against Amaya's stomach and listen, giggling, talking about how strong the heartbeat was, and how special the child would be with them to raise him. She insisted it was a boy. Amaya dreaded having a son all the more because he might grow up to be like the brute who'd raped her. What was worse, she knew she'd used him and was in part responsible. This growing squirming creature made her want to squirm too but she could see no way out.

~ * ~

As the months passed, Joumi began to despair more and more of ever finding Amaya. Tokyo teemed with people. He wondered if she'd not gotten herself an American patron, and sometimes went to Little America to look for her. Of course it was hopeless. All he saw were American jeeps, American faces, American cars, and American eateries. If she *was* here, he did not think he would ever be able to forgive her.

He regularly went to her flat and assumed payment of the rent. He'd had the couch removed and replaced it with another one. Maybe she'd come back here. She could not know Briton was dead though, and he hoped she'd never want to come here again. Because if she returned, he feared it would be out of need, and what a horror for her to think she must resume what surely had been despicable. Joumi only needed to look around at other Japanese girls ensconced with Westerners to know they did what they did not out of love but because many of these guys provided for them, at least until they went home and forgot them.

One day Joumi stretched out on the new couch in her sitting room remembering how tender their times together were and how special the future had promised to be. He took the relic out of the pocket in his kimono. It was brittle and dried, an ear the thugs had cut off and sent to him months back. At first, when he'd received it, he'd been glad Briton was food for sharks, but looking at the shriveled remains, he knew he needed to get rid of it and move on with his life. He understood why he carried such a thing with him, though. It was a constant reminder to himself that *he* was alive and so was Amaya, *somewhere*, and there must be some way for them to reconnect.

~ * ~

Amaya's son was born above the Kabuki Theater. It was not physically a hard delivery, but emotionally it was crushing. Junko paid a midwife to help. The woman cut the umbilical cord and put the crying infant on Amaya's chest. It had a shock of black hair and a very red face. Amaya did not want to give the baby her breast, but she was dripping with milk and when the infant screamed, her body reacted. She let him suck. She hated him, and wanted to push him away from her body, but there was Junko cooing and smiling, with nappies ready and a baby blanket she'd crocheted.

"What shall we call him?" Junko asked. She'd wanted to name him for her father, and Amaya almost said yes, but her brother's name jumped out of her mouth. "He shall be called Haruo."

Junko smiled and did not argue. She knew Haruo meant the world to Amaya who'd been learning to play the shamisen so she could go to Hiroshima to find him. "Haruo is perfect," Junko murmured, and gently took the baby after he'd stopped feeding. She wrapped him in a silk sheet. "You are so precious," she purred.

Amaya lay awake all night wanting to kill this half-breed who would never stop reminding her not only of the rape but also that she'd lost Joumi, and her chances of becoming an actress were over. Why should *he* live and her life be finished?

Early in the morning, she crept out of bed, careful not to wake Junko who was on her back, snoring gently. Amaya looked lovingly at the face of this woman who'd become like a mother to her. She almost relented, but she'd made up her mind. She'd hoped she could bond with the kid once it was born, and her desire to put it to death would disappear, but it hadn't, and now she felt as if she had no choice. "I am so sorry, Junko," she whispered.

Her heart broke as she carried the infant nestled against her chest and made her way down the narrow stairs and out the door. It was bewildering to be outside after nine months never feeling rain or sun or snow. She looked at the buildings around her in the early morning. How good it would be to be free once again. Free of all burdens. She began to walk glad nobody was about except her.

~ * ~

Joumi groaned, hardly able to sleep. He'd suddenly lost his confidence in the Flying Feathers. He doubted they would become a worldwide phenomenon, and though he still had diamonds, what good were they? He needed to find a way to get his investment back, but he hated to leave Suminoe Works in the lurch. He might be wrong, but his premonition haunted him. His bad luck seemed to him to be coupled with his despair over Amaya who'd never been out of his mind for more than moments. Today, he must stop his foolish waiting. Today the apartment where he'd so often gone to sit and dream about holding her was being let to someone else. All the furniture had been sold, even her sleeping mat. He'd kept her clothes and her teapot as reminders of what might have been. No other woman would ever do, but he knew even in reduced circumstances, he was still a catch. He still had resources and he would re-invent himself in a new business.

He splashed water on his face and prepared for his day, putting on a kimono and tying a thin green belt around his waist. He'd lost weight. What if *she* had starved? He held his head in his hands, trying to dispel this ugly notion. How easily he could have taken care of her. Why had he been so stupid? *No good to go back and blame himself. No good.* One more time, he decided, he would go for a final look, one final search of Ginza Street, and a walk along the poor section he'd driven her through when they'd first met. She'd been so stunning, looking every bit a talented Geisha, only much better, because she'd been cheeky and able to spar with him verbally and there had been such a spark between them. *No,* he told himself. *I must not go back there. It is over.* But he could not help himself and even though it was very early, drove over and waited in his car fifty feet away from the doors to the apartment building.

~ * ~

It was a couple of miles back to her old flat. Every step wore Amaya out but she couldn't turn back. Once Amaya saw the building, she began to shake. Junko advised her to never go there. Amaya knew her friend spoke out of love and concern. *Dear Junko,* she thought, *I will make things up to you. I will make you understand this is for the best. He is the father.* The baby felt heavy in her arms but at least he hadn't cried and demanded milk. She didn't think she could give another ounce of herself.

The apartment building looked like the same old brown brick with rugs and undergarments hanging over the railings, with bicycles lining the curb, and with the Imperial dragons guarding the doorway. Every step closer made her heart beat faster. What if he raped her again? What if he was not there? She truly hoped he wasn't but then what would she do with this child?

The baby gripped her hair and tugged. She gently released his little fingers, but one look at his innocent face caused a pang that took her breath away. Gasping, she clutched the baby and ran away from the flats as fast as she could, finding herself at the very shrine where she'd once prayed to Amida to bring Joumi back to her. She sank to the floor. The hole in the roof was repaired now with thatch so it was dry inside. There was still no statue of the Buddha, but Amaya needed not something made of stone. She needed some deep spirit to stir her and move her and free her. Amaya did not know what to do. She had been unable to bring herself to enter the apartment building. She did not want to go back to Junko who would insist they keep the child. Amaya could not, *would not*, raise this baby no matter how hard it was to let him go. And it was harder than she'd possibly imagined all those months carrying him, wishing him dead. But here he was, living flesh of her flesh. He did not look white, and that was a comfort. He might truly resemble Haruo.

She stroked the small red face and opened her blouse to give him her breast. "I won't starve you," she whispered. "Your father," and she shuddered, "loved his children in England. Perhaps *he* will take you back there and you will have brothers and sisters to take care of you and play with you. Lucy, his wife, is probably kind. She will take you in."

Amaya knew this was impossible. She knew plenty of girls who had half-caste babies that no one wanted on either side of the ocean. Her heart sank for this child. Perhaps she ought to keep him. With Junko she could make a decent life for the boy, perhaps even give him a chance to go to university when he grew up.

Amaya shook away these remorseful and hopeful ideas, rebuttoned her blouse, burped the child, and stood up, staring back the way she'd come. "It must be done," she muttered. "I must be brave." She pretended she was an actress returning a baby she had stolen, telling herself how happy the real mother would be to get back her infant.

When she turned onto her street, she saw a car pulling away, driving slowing toward Ginza, and she thought it must be Joumi. She yearned to run after him, but surely it could not really be *he*. Why would he come here? *How foolish I am*, she thought. She walked up to the entrance of the apartment building but it loomed above her, reminding her of unbearable memories. Unable to enter, she made her way back to the shrine where she gently laid the baby on the floor, wrapping him securely in the silk sheet. He began to bawl. Tears laced her face, but she turned her back and walked away.

Ten

Amaya did not go far from the shrine. She wanted to flee and forget everything, including the helpless baby, but some instinct within her breast, some deep maternal responsibility made her turn around. She hid at the side of a ramshackle house not far away. It looked as if no one lived here, but even such ruins as this one with its caved-in roof and shattered walls might be a place of refuge for some homeless soul.

It seemed an age that she waited, and it began to rain. She had no umbrella and was soon soaked through. She silently thanked whoever had taken care of the roof of the shrine that the baby was dry. No one came, not even a single child out to play. Amaya began to fret. As the rain became a deluge, she imagined she heard the infant bawling and she could hardly breathe. She wondered who owned this shrine. Many temples were maintained by rich families, or at least people who used to be rich. That was when she had a better idea.

Her wet clothes clung to her skinny body, but she did not hesitate. She didn't care if she caught pneumonia. She retrieved the child, who was resting peacefully, perhaps soothed to sleep by the thudding rain upon the thatch. Water dripped from the eaves and she was careful to make sure the child was not dampened. She refused to look at his little face. The warmth from his small body filled her, but she pretended not to notice.

Walking briskly, she soon reached Ginza Street and found the traffic humming with people filling the shops. She realized it was already mid-morning, but it felt as if a lifetime had flashed before her eyes. The trolley she caught took her directly to the Imperial Palace. There was no way to enter, but she crossed the double bridge over the moat and put the baby on the ground near the gates, off to one side where he wouldn't be run over, but most likely be seen.

She retreated, trying not to look back, but once again she was unable to just leave him there, and so she hunkered down at the far end of the bridge aware she must look homeless in her wet garments with her saturated hair hanging limply down her back. It did not matter to her what anyone thought. When a limousine drove across the bridge, and someone got out to open the gate, she wanted to cry out. She wanted to say *no, no, no*, but her voice stuck in her throat.

She heard a guttural sound from the driver and saw him pick the baby up and hold him in front of his chest, examining him. *Be careful with his head,* she wanted to yell. *His name is Haruo.* She turned and shuffled away before anyone could question her.

She did not know how she could face Junko now, and she did not know how she could live with herself, but it was done. The child was in the care of rich people who would surely do what was right. Since the baby was a boy they might well have him adopted into a family who needed a son. He might have a prosperous life, be given an education. After all, this was the palace of the Emperor. He would not let the child or her down. Would he?

~ * ~

Joumi parked his car and wandered along Ginza, staring for a brief time at the Waco building where he'd first been mesmerized by Amaya. Trolleys rumbled past. He little knew that upon one of them Amaya had recently sat slumped over her infant, trying not to weep. Some strange stirring caused him to shake his head trying to deny the unseen force prodding him, telling him to look inside a bus. He not look. Instead, he sorrowfully decided he must do something to cheer himself up. He wandered along Ginza to the Kabuki Theater. He hadn't been here since it was reconstructed and it would do him good to see a play. He checked the schedule. There was an evening performance of Tsuri Onna, a play written in 1902 about two men fishing for wives. Joumi almost walked away. He did not think he could bear to watch this silly show about foolish guys. *He* felt so foolish. Perhaps this was an opportunity to exorcise the ghost of Amaya forever. He managed to buy a ticket, almost choking upon being handed only one when he so wanted two.

The theater was crowded with people sitting on benches, sipping saké and tea. The performance got underway with two actors wearing colorful kimonos entering the stage, and bowing to the audience. One was a Lord, but clearly the other, a servant, seemed to be leading him by the nose. They went to a shrine to pray for a perfect bride. Joumi pondered this scene thinking maybe he should go to a temple to pray about Amaya, but he'd never been religious. He did not think he could start now. Besides he'd made the decision to move on with his life.

The Lord, in the play, cast out his fishing line into the pond and reeled in a beautiful girl clad all in white. He immediately asked for her hand and was accepted. Joumi felt so sad, but found himself laughing with the audience when the servant fished for *his* wife and instead of a gorgeous maiden, a very ugly woman in a garish kimono jumped onto him and clung fiercely with her hands around his neck. Joumi told himself perhaps he'd had a lucky escape.

As he left the theater walking slowly to his car, he realized he'd quite enjoyed himself and vowed he would come more often to the theater.

~ * ~

Amaya did not return to the Kabuki Theater that night. She could not face Junko, and instead went to Girl's place, enduring, from behind a screen, the agony of listening to her friend pretend hot sex with various GIs. She did not divulge why she was in such a mess, but Girl was too busy to ask questions.

When morning came, she gave Amaya hot tea and a pastry. Amaya pushed it away. "Thank you, Girl, but I can't eat. I am not hungry."

"You are too thin," Girl retorted. "Eat."

Amaya obeyed, eating silently while Girl watched her. "We best friends?" Girl asked.

"Always," Amaya said quietly.

"So where you been the last nine months? You have a baby, didn't you? Don't lie. I can tell by the way you been holding your stomach. I can see you hurting. Where is the kid? Why didn't you come to me? I've been to your flat. No one there but your sweetheart Joumi. Why'd you not keep his child, maybe even marry the guy?"

Amaya felt overwhelming shame and wanted to lie, but if anyone would understand what she'd done, it would be Girl. Amaya looked up, her face flaming. "I couldn't keep him. He's not Joumi's." Suddenly, she realized what Girl had said. "What do you mean Joumi was in my flat? When?"

"It must have been him unless your English jerk is tall, thin Japanese. Is he?"

"I don't want to talk about *him*." Amaya hissed the words.

Girl nodded. "What happened? He come back and give you baby?"

Amaya was flooded with horror remembering what had happened. "It doesn't matter. The child will be well taken care of."

Girl shrugged. "Maybe. More than likely your half breed will end up in the river."

Amaya felt herself flush with anger. "I named him Haruo," she said defensively.

"What?" Girl responded. "You think naming him after your brother will protect him? You think he grow up to become a man of spring like his name, coming to life after winter. This kid you abandoned he not have a good life. Trust me."

Amaya hung her head. She politely thanked Girl for the tea, the food, and the overnight accommodations such as they had been. She quickly went her way determined she would see to it her child would not be neglected. *Junko will help me*, she thought, but her fingers trembled. She'd betrayed Junko's trust. Junko might be small in size, but Amaya suspected her fury would be mighty. She would have every right to turn Amaya away.

Amaya made her way back to the theater and crept up the steep stairs into the attic. She could hear voices from Junko's quarters behind the screens, and stood still, listening. It was her Kabuki actor friend in the attic trying to console Junko. "It was her kid. You have to let her do what she wants with her own child even if she wants to drown it like a rat."

Amaya felt shame sink her to the ground but upon hearing Junko groan mournfully, she managed to stand up and walk toward their voices. She peeked around the lattice frame.

"You!" Junko exploded and rushed toward her and dragged her into the room. "Where is Haruo?"

"I am sorry, Junko." Amaya could not look Junko in the face.

"We were going to raise him," Junko cried and stared accusingly at Amaya. "Even if you didn't want him, I would have kept him."

"I just couldn't. You know why. I told you what happened. I know it's not the baby's fault. I know."

Junko remained silent.

The young actor patted her on her shoulder and, looking embarrassed, took his leave, bowing his way out of the room.

"Junko," Amaya pleaded. "I don't blame you for being angry with me, but if there's any way, I want to make sure the baby is well-placed. I don't know how," she wailed. "What shall I do?"

Junko grunted. "I will see to it. Tell me again exactly where you left him."

"Promise me you won't bring him here." Even as Amaya spoke these words, she wished Junko would ignore them. But somehow she knew Junko would be true to her word. She told her where she'd left the baby and how a man from a limo had picked him up.

"I will take money and a note to the palace." Junko shook her head. "Then it's up to the gods."

~ * ~

When Joumi read in the paper about the baby found at the Palace gates, he almost fainted. The infant's name was Haruo. That was Amaya's brother's name. Could it be possible that Amaya had given birth to a son? He began to perspire with hope. Maybe he could find her. There must be a lead.

It was not easy to get an audience with any of the Palace officials, but he bribed a few people. At last, he went to meet with a low-placed clerk for a drink. The man had a fat belly and a too-smiling demeanor for Joumi's taste. He also wore Western clothing, easy to spot in the Japanese restaurant where they met.

They bowed politely and sank onto low benches, waiting for the waiter to bring them a pot of tea.

Joumi poured. "I am trying to find the mother of the infant left at the palace," he muttered, observing the palace servant over the rim of his tea cup.

The other man nodded.

"Where is the child now?" Joumi asked, suddenly thinking perhaps if he saw the baby, he would know for sure if it belonged to Amaya.

"He's been placed in care at a temple. No idea which one. Monks will see he is adopted out. That's all I know."

"There must be something else…"

"There is one thing. A cleaning lady saw who left the money."

Joumi despaired. He'd not known about any money. How could he possibly hope to find one woman amongst the millions in Tokyo? He knew his face showed his despair.

The man held out his hand. "What I know is worth something?"

Joumi, sick of paying bribes, felt like punching this fellow, but he obligingly took out his wallet and gave the man a hundred yen. "That is all I will give you. Now, tell me what you know."

"I didn't see him myself. I only heard about him. It might not be true, but if it is..."

Joumi felt like getting up and walking away. Probably this guy was making things up to extort more money. It crossed Joumi's mind to contact the thugs who'd gotten rid of Briton and have them take care of this crook. "What might or might not be true?" he asked, exasperated.

"It was a dwarf, so I heard. A little person, and not Japanese either. That should narrow things down." He smirked, pocketed the money, slurped the remainder of his tea, and hurried away into the street, fast disappearing into the crowd of people.

Eleven

What at first seemed a lead that must surely take him to Amaya created more hell. The first dwarfs Joumi found out about were a couple who lived above a brothel, cleaned the house, and cooked for the girls. They did not want to speak to him and vehemently denied knowing of any money given to the palace. The door slammed in his face. Joumi shook his head, wondering why they were so nasty. Perhaps they'd been persecuted, but more than likely even in the worst militaristic purges back in the thirties, these people hadn't even been born. It seemed unlikely they'd been communists, but perhaps their parents were. Who knew?

A week later his contacts sent him to a guy who'd somehow managed to earn enough dosh to convert his flat to suit his small stature. Joumi stooped to enter and crouched uncomfortably near a miniature chair, aware of the erotic paintings on the walls of women who looked like dolls next to men with huge penises. It made him wonder how difficult it must be to have a body everyone stared at, some with compassion perhaps, but most with contempt or indifference. Joumi felt rising horror, wondering if this guy pimped women, but he did not let on how uncomfortable he felt. "I am looking for a woman," he began, and hesitated at this guy's smirk. "Not for sex. She had a baby," and he unaccountably added. "*My* baby. I want to marry her, but she ran away. A dwarf left money at the palace to take care of the child. Was it you?"

"Me?" the fellow chortled. "I don't deal in pregnant girls." The man grinned lasciviously. "I haven't seen your woman. I certainly wouldn't give money to rich people. Good luck in finding your chick."

The next person he heard about in the paper was an actor in a theatrical troupe who toured the country, singing and dancing. His hopes rose. It was quite possible Amaya would know people in the theater and even if she didn't know them, she'd be drawn to actors and actresses. Once again, when this troupe finally arrived back in Tokyo after having been touring seaside resorts, he was disappointed. "I am looking for someone small like you, possibly a foreigner, who left a baby at the palace," Joumi said, trying to be respectful. He bent down and looked deeply into the man's clear eyes.

The guy grinned. "The Emperor has never sought to employ me," he said, "not even to wipe his ass. Let alone take me into his confidence."

"Do you know of any foreign-born dwarfs?" Joumi continued, desperate and hopeful this friendly fellow might point him in the right direction.

"Can't say that I do," he replied. "Sorry. If I hear of anyone, I'll let you know."

Joumi bowed and began to leave.

"Try the circus," the dwarf called after him. "Lot of my people get jobs as freaks."

Joumi gave him a wry smile and shook his head. "Do not belittle yourself," he said, and realizing the term he'd used might give offence, quickly added, "Stature is of no importance. You are a good man. Thank you for your help."

It seemed utterly hopeless to try to find one person, no matter how different he might look, in a population of over six hundred thousand people, all crammed into one city, much of which was still in chaos. Too, it was quite possible this particular dwarf did not live in Tokyo. Perhaps Amaya had chosen someone at random to deliver the money to care for the infant.

Joumi, wanting to raise his spirits, decided to treat himself to another Kabuki play, the famous Churshingura, which told the tale of forty-seven Samurai who committed mass suicide. When he was a boy, Joumi used to enjoy this show performed by puppets. He'd believed those Samurai who'd killed themselves were brave. Now, watching real men in their ceremonial kimonos on the Kabuki stage slash their guts made him want to cry. It was only with great effort he did not break down entirely. As a boy, the atonement of the Samurai for what they considered their dishonorable act of murder seemed brave and noble, but now all he could think was how meaningless life seemed without Amaya to love. He already felt dead inside, so perhaps *he* ought to kill himself.

The play, quite an extravaganza with many actors drew to a close. They came on stage and bowed. People applauded and soon began to get up and exit the theater. A few were laughing, clearly having enjoyed a cup of wine. Others seemed somber. Joumi remained seated, forcing the people on his bench to climb over him. No one complained. Could they sense his agony? *So much planning,* he thought ruefully, *to wreak vengeance.* He felt as if he were a hundred years old, and not a man in his prime who could still conquer the world and restore his wealth. His head drooped and he covered his eyes, unwilling to get up and leave even though almost everyone else was gone.

For the first time in his life, so it seemed, he felt humbled and unable to cope. He wished he *might* die but knew he'd never have the courage to take his own life. He remembered how relieved he'd been when he'd been assigned as a POW guard, and how ashamed he'd felt about his gladness that he wasn't forced to fly a plane into an enemy warship. Joumi felt on fire with shame and regret. He wished he might be struck down by a warrior, but he wanted no one to come near him either. An unbidden prayer formed in his mind. It was simple and seemed not to be from him. "Help," he moaned.

"Theater's closing," a janitor who was cleaning up told him. "You can't stay here."

Joumi looked up. "I'm sorry," he muttered and a strange impulse took hold of him. "I'd like to go backstage and meet the actors." He almost hoped one of the Samurai would be a real warrior and cut him down, but of course he knew he was being ridiculous.

"Try number six. That guy likes to talk to his fans," the janitor told him, sweeping up the crumbs from cakes people had eaten during the show. "Door is on left of stage."

Joumi nodded his thanks and slowly made his way to the back of the playhouse and hesitated. He felt exhausted. He ought to go home and console himself with a glass of beer, not go back to do what? *Ask some Kabuki Samurai to slay him and end his miserable existence?* At last he made up his mind. He *would* go back and thank an actor for his superb performance. They were amazing, and perhaps thanking one person would help him feel better about himself. Their performance released feelings he hadn't known he had about war, about suicide, and about his own failings which he knew to be many. It was important to be self-aware. He stepped through the doorway and made his way down a corridor with many doors leading into dressing rooms. He stood outside one, listening to tired and excited voices from inside. It was no good. He had nothing to say. Even his *thank you* seemed contrived, not for anyone's benefit but his own.

Before he had a chance to leave, the door opened and a strange person looked up at him.

At first he thought it must be a child, but there were no kids in the play. This face was old and too large for its body. Joumi's throat constricted. A dwarf! With a Korean face—but not a man, a *woman* in a flowery kimono.

"You want to see Kira Kozukenosuke or you want to pick a fight with Asano?" she quipped.

Joumi stared rudely. "You," he finally muttered. "You are a dwarf."

"What of it?" the woman bristled and brushed past him. "You need to go home, mister."

"Wait," Joumi cried. "Is Amaya here?"

The dwarf turned around and offered him her hand. "So, Joumi, you have found us."

"Found you?" Joumi took the small hand which shook his firmly. "You know my name?" His heart beat so hard he thought his chest would explode.

"Sure," the lady said. "I'm Junko. And no, Amaya is not here. Sorry. She told me about you." Junko turned her back, hurried away, disappearing up the stairs.

Joumi stood there stupefied.

"Come on," the dwarf called. "You'd better come with me. I'll get you a stiff drink."

~ * ~

Amaya, far away in Hiroshima, slipped out of her delicate pink sandals with leather thongs, leaving them in the small agari-kamachi behind the sliding paper doors that led into the room where she was to sleep. Her host, a sturdy fellow with a handsome face, even if too broad as all Korean faces seemed, wore paper slippers. He took her bags into her quarters and went to the far end of the room. He tapped a closet with one toe. "Sleeping futons are in here. I believe you will find them comfortable. My wife insists upon soft mattresses. There are blankets and pillows in there too."

Amaya gave a tiny smile of thanks and followed him into a glassed-in sitting area where he laid her luggage on a low wooden table. "Please rest and in about an hour join us for refreshments. We are looking forward to learning more about you. Sonja, my wife, is anxious to learn how Junko is doing these days."

Her hosts were cousins of Junko's. The guy, Bae Sahng, was a physician who'd worked at Hiroshima Hospital before it was destroyed by the A-bomb. Fortunately he'd been on holiday with his family the day of the attack. The bomb detonated right above the building with the blast directed downward.

It hardly bore thinking how many patients were incinerated, but Amaya knew more than eighty people died instantly. She groaned to herself remembering the people she'd seen at the station, now under reconstruction. These people might have survived but their disfiguring scars looked disgusting, and their eyes seemed full of humiliation as if they'd done something evil. *Not they,* she thought, *who are evil. You are. Deserting your brother, deserting your child.*

Amaya paced. The room was not luxurious but decent, and free. It certainly wasn't a real Ryokan Guest House but a single room specially converted for visitors. The tatami mat beneath her feet felt a little rough, not of the best quality, but it was a wonder anyone could afford anything, especially here. She grabbed a newspaper from a stack neatly folded on a shelf inside the tokonoma which also contained a vase filled with dried flowers, alongside a ceremonial knife. Its rusty stained blade made her shudder. She read the latest statistics about how many people had survived, but if the writer intended to fill people with hope, with her he did not succeed. These numbers chilled her. It seemed impossible. No one she knew wanted to remember what happened, but for some reason someone had underlined the statistics. How glad could anyone feel about the one-hundred-fifty-eight-thousand people who'd survived the first attack in Hiroshima? Their lives must have continued to be hell.

She could not imagine how they'd suffered, did

not want to think about it, yet she hoped she might find her brother, Haruo, amongst the living, maybe even in the rebuilt hospital where she was expecting to entertain patients. Dr. Sahng was going to arrange matters. She threw the paper down and picked up the shamisen she'd bought along. She'd practiced tirelessly and although she did not feel proficient with the instrument, she could manage a few popular tunes. After playing a few chords, she gave up and resumed pacing, at last coming to a halt in front of a mirror.

How thin she'd become, her luminous eyes shining sadly back at her, reminding her of the overwhelming sadness she could not rid herself of. Even the red and white flowers on her kimono looked *too* pretty. At least the wide black obi around her waist made her appear shapely. Perhaps she could pretend she'd never given birth, but even if no one could see beneath the cloth, her belly sagged and her breasts still ached, as if every cell in her body viscerally remembered her son, now five months old. She would not think about him now. She'd come to be a help and a comfort to others, and she could not deny she hoped this would warm the coldness that seemed to fill every pore of her being.

Later, she found her way to a dining room where tea was already set out and the older couple sat waiting for her. They smiled and stood, bowing to her, offering her a cushion near the square table that filled the center of the small room. In a gracious move, she lowered herself near the table. She'd expected Junko's family to be dwarfs too, but the wife was tall and thin and very pretty. "Thank you for letting me stay with you," Amaya said, accepting a cup of green tea and sipping it slowly, enjoying its bitter taste. "Junko told me you work at the hospital, Dr. Sangh," Amaya said, wanting to get straight to the point.

"Please call me Bae. We both work at the medical center. Sonja is a nurse. Before we talk of such matters, tell us how is my wife's cousin, Junko? Her parents died, you know, and we couldn't find her."

Sonja's face flushed and she looked away.

It occurred to Amaya they had *not* tried hard to find Junko and help her probably because she was a dwarf whose parents were foreign workers who'd died of overwork and lack of food. Looking at these two earnest people, a doctor and a nurse who spent their days saving lives, their fingers rigidly gripping their cups, Amaya felt sorry for them It surely must have been hard for them to be third-world persons even if they did have good jobs as respectable hospital staff. "Junko is very well. She is happy and enjoys working in the Kabuki Theater where she has lots of friends." Amaya smiled at them warmly. "She is a wonderful woman. Without her, I would be dead." She turned the conversation. "You must also have helped many people."

"We have tried our best. It has been very hard here with so little food," the doctor said. "Many people died of starvation. Tokyo too must have been hard-hit after the war ended." He nodded as if deciding to go on. "Japanese people are my people too but many atrocities occurred and brought such wrath upon us. Horrible, horrible."

Amaya waited for him to continue but he seemed lost in thought. "All that is over now," she said, but she wanted to cry, wanted to ask if it was possible her brother might be among the living. Perhaps this man would know.

"It is not finished for many," he said, and noticing her glum face, seemed to feel as if he'd insulted her, and with his following words, obviously wanted to make amends. "Very many Japanese are also heroes," he said gently. "Do you know of Dr. Kaoru Shima? He came back immediately after the bomb fell. He opposed the war, I can tell you. Thank God he was away that day. He is a miracle worker. The very day after he got back, he searched the rubble of the hospital building. My wife, who is a nurse, can tell you…"

His wife lowered her eyes. "He found an operating instrument he'd bought in the United States where he got his medical training. Can you imagine! It had survived. It was a sign of hope for us. It was a miracle."

"It could not have gotten any worse," her husband interrupted. "You forget the corpses."

"No," she said somberly. "I will never forget." She looked at Amaya. "In the ruins we found skeletons, their bones bleached white from the blast, every ounce of flesh gone."

"It must have been awful," Amaya cried, remembering her brother had lost both legs.

"Yes. It was very bad. Dr. Shima hoped to find survivors. But the hospital was at the epicenter. He propped a message board against a fire cistern outside the debris, wanting to alert anyone seeking their families, but not one person ever contacted him. All dead."

Amaya could not stop the tears welling up. "My brother, Haruo," she managed to squeak. "He made it, but he lost both his legs. I left him in a hospital run by the Americans. I heard he was transferred to Shima. Could you help me find him?"

Both their faces clouded. "He is probably gone, but we will look in the hospital records. With so many wounded, and so much chaos, it is unlikely he'd have got to stay in the hospital for long. He would have been discharged, unless he died."

Amaya did not want to hear any more. She so wanted Haruo to be alive even if he was permanently disabled. She wanted to bring him home with her, except she didn't have a home to speak of, and knew she could not stay with Junko much longer.

Twelve

Joumi could not believe his luck. He'd managed to withdraw his investment from the Flying Feathers without much loss of his funds. He'd thought these light-weight fuel-efficient cars ahead of their time, but he'd realized people didn't want economy these days. They wanted a restoration to former grandeur. That, he doubted, would ever happen, but he was happy to put his money into another company called Nissan which bought engines from Suminoe, the manufacturer of the Feathers. He couldn't explain it in rational terms but he knew Nissan was going to make him a lot of money in the future. He need but wait. Even better, he need not wait any longer to find Amaya. He knew she was in Hiroshima staying with Junko's cousins. Sure, Junko tried to dissuade him from going after her, questioning him, and demanding to know what made him think Amaya would want him?

He didn't know if she would. He'd told Junko

as much but he had no intention of paying attention to her pleas to let Amaya stay in Hiroshima. Radiation might still be a danger. He wanted to bring her back to Tokyo. He knew she might reject men forever but he was determined to woo her and love her and beg her to consent to become his wife. He didn't want her to marry him out of need or greed or opportunism. He decided to tell her he feared he'd lost all his money, and how he would make much more in the future and hoped she could trust him and rely upon him.

In high spirits he drove along a narrow, winding road toward Hiroshima. He patted the top pocket in his double-breasted suit, making sure the note with the address of Junko's cousins was safe. His hope mingled with anxiety. She might reject him permanently. He would not think such negative thoughts. He would find a way to restore their relationship and deepen it, in a way she could not resist. He even considered finding her infant and telling her he would raise the boy as his own, but he was not sure she'd find such an offer irresistible. If he couldn't find the kid, she'd be more let down than ever. He did not want to do that to her. He knew she must have very confused feelings about this baby.

When he arrived in Hiroshima, his heart sank as he went past a cemetery so crowded with gravestones it hardly had enough room for the skeletons beneath the soil, let alone corpses, but perhaps all that remained was ashes. He pulled over and stopped and stared over the graveyard at new buildings. They looked modern and out of touch with the decay and death all around them. The plain walls and solid roof appeared strong but lacked the beauty of Japanese architecture. For some reason, although he did not favor religion, he felt as if there ought to be a temple here with a Pagoda roof, Buddha icons, and pretty gardens.

Beyond a distant wall, he could see gleaming mountains.

Amaya might be looking this very moment at the same horizon, he thought. He started up his car, looked at his map, and resumed his journey, knowing he was minutes away from arriving. Unless Amaya had left already, but he had it on Junko's good word that she'd recently gotten a letter from her cousin explaining how sad they'd been to discover Amaya's brother had died of leukemia, but she seemed to be holding up well. She was invited to play her shamisen and sing at a performance to commemorate the planting of the peace tree. Joumi remembered when it was in the papers about this tree sapling that survived the blast. Already, three years had passed since it became a symbol of harmony.

Joumi wondered whether or not to immediately go to Amaya, or should he wait until the concert and listen to her play and see her dance? Undecided but full of longing, he drove into the district where Amaya was staying and cruised by the house, pleased to see it intact and respectable. Not good enough for her, of course, because he planned to build her a castle. Why, if she wanted moats, she would have them. If she wanted a shrine, that too he would provide for her. But what if she told him no?

He could not bear such a thought and found himself driving another twenty five minutes further and getting on the ferry to the Miyajima Hills. As the boat glided across the choppy water, he stared at the grand gate of the Itsukushima Shrine, its red pillars rising elegantly from the depths of the sea, its curved green roof glistening in front of a sky purple with clouds. A solitary bird perched on one end of the central beam. He could not explain even to himself his urgent need to prostrate himself in front of the Buddha, but this gate commanded respect. He suspected it was simply superstitious of him, but it comforted him to think if he had the help of a power beyond himself, things would surely work out for the best. He wished he could throw himself physically onto the deck of the ferry. Too many others were crowded onto the boat. Instead, he tried to humble his mind and became aware of how powerless he actually felt. He remembered when he'd muttered *help* at the Kabuki Theater how he had immediately found Junko. Perhaps there *was* an infinite power. It gave him hope.

~ * ~

Amaya accepted the letter from Junko's cousin, Bae, and waited for him to leave her room, but he stood silently waiting for her to open it.

"It's from Junko," he said, expectantly. "I recognize her writing."

"Yes," Amaya responded. "She has such a neat hand with such tiny print, so precious." She tried to figure how to politely say she wanted to read her letter alone, and if there was anything of interest for her hosts, she would tell them. Instead, she stepped backward and with a curt nod, not intended to be insulting but probably so, inquired, "Bae, didn't Junko send you a note too?"

The doctor cleared his throat. "No," he said. "I do not mean to pry."

Amaya heard his wife's kimono sweep along the corridor and the sound of a door quietly sliding closed.

"Please, if we can be of assistance, let us know." He began to leave.

Amaya felt chastened. "You are such a big help to me. You and Sonja. I can never thank you enough. I promise to let you know how Junko is, but I suspect she is writing to me about personal matters."

"Of course," the stately elder man said and quietly turned and went into his bedroom.

Amaya comforted her rudeness, aware that she was tired after spending time visiting children with radiation poisoning in the hospital. She'd made silly jokes and tickled them and hugged them, telling them how beautiful they were, but those knowing eyes haunted her. Their bald heads, their skinny bodies, some with swollen abdomens, some with horrific burns, broke her heart. She didn't want to remember the healthy baby boy she'd rejected. She didn't want to give in to sentiment, but these little children, all of them orphans, tore at her resolve.

At last, after carefully slitting the letter open with the ceremonial knife, she began to read. In these first moments before she could understand a word, she shook with the memory of the letter she'd had from Ben Briton and what had resulted.

This letter was from Junko. Amaya refused to give in to recollection of that which was past, determined to let go of the agony of recall. Her eyes perused the words and her heart began to race. Junko had told Joumi where she was. Junko, after dropping this bombshell, couched in criticism of all men, and yet raising Joumi up as a potential husband, chattered about the theater telling of who had argued with whom and how the latest play had gone. Her friend's final apologies seemed misplaced. Yet Amaya was happy to think Joumi might show up. She found herself smiling at Junko's disingenuous strategy to get her back with Joumi. Would he come, she wondered?

Amaya lay awake half the night on her futon. Her brother was long dead, now she knew. It grieved her but not so much. Many years had passed and to know he was no longer suffering came as a relief. Still, she blamed herself, but only because she wished she had been with him when he'd died. The thought of him being all alone was unbearable. She considered how she did not deserve anyone to love her. Joumi must be a fool. If he knew about the child, or ever found out, he would surely discard her like an old shoe.

Yet, a little hope flared. It would be so wonderful to be in the arms of the man she loved and had always loved from the moment she'd first seen his lanky body in the Ginza building at the Yank's party. He wanted her too, she knew. How foolish of him to be so jealous and to have ruined their time together.

How things might be so different. The child she'd borne might have been his.

It hurt to think about baby Haruo, but he no longer belonged to her. As far as she was concerned, the infant was as dead as her brother. It was too late to change anything, too late for regrets, but not so easy to lay aside her interior sorrow no matter how bright a face she put on, no matter how sweet her voice sounded singing to the delicate strings of the shamisen. Amaya held the ceremonial knife above her chest as if she were Samurai about to plunge it into her heart. She could not help but wonder if the rusty blade had ever been used. It was antique, yet still sharp enough to cut. She ran it across her stomach, ripping the nightie she wore, pondering what it would be like to die and wishing she could end her uncertainty, her confusion, and her guilt.

~ * ~

Joumi wanted to turn around and go immediately back to the mainland, but he'd missed the last ferry and so he had no choice but to book into a hotel. His restlessness kept him awake half the night. He couldn't believe he'd not stopped at the house where Amaya lived. She might slip through his hands again. It would be his stupid fault. What impulse prevented him from simply knocking on the door? What fear held him back? He realized as he lay sweating on his sleeping mat that fear rendered him incapable of taking the risk, and he wondered if his insane jealousy of Ebisu had also been a way to prevent genuine intimacy with Amaya.

He'd spent most of his life feeling coldly alone and filling that emptiness with work, success, money, and whores. None of it worked for long or gave him any deep satisfaction. *Surely*, he cried in his mind, *there is more to life than this constant suffering, this longing that is never quenched.* Religion, so far as he was concerned, had been a way to keep people ignorant and easily controlled and manipulated, but a feeling almost like a moth at a lamp persisted. He did, of course, ignore it.

~ * ~

Amaya knew she could never commit suicide with a sword. She put the ceremonial knife back on its shelf, and got up. She washed and refreshed her hair. Putting on her best kimono, she surveyed herself in the mirror but the image she saw seemed ugly. Joumi would not want her. No one would. She did not want herself. Yes, she'd told herself it had been a relief her brother's suffering was over, and she'd told herself the baby named for him, baby Haruo, was dead to her, and besides he'd been placed in a good home, but what if he weren't in a good home? What if he were being abused, his little legs being slashed by a cane? Who would bring back her brother?

She left early in the morning without taking tea, careful not to wake her hosts, tiptoeing in bare feet out the door. Stones dug into the bottoms of her feet but she took no notice. She limped toward distant mountains unaware of most of her surroundings, except she noticed many gravestones, gray in the early light, crammed together near a plain brick building. She stopped and rubbed her feet. Perhaps Haruo's corpse lay rotting under the dirt in this place, under one of the unmarked stones, his flesh stinking, his soul unwanted, his loss never properly mourned.

There will be no gravestone for me, she thought, and for a brief moment felt sad to be letting Junko down again, Junko who'd given her back her life. Junko no longer wanted her around. Clearly Junko hoped Joumi might marry her and then she'd be off Junko's hands. Dear Junko. She'd so wanted the baby.

There was no going back.

Amaya came at last, her feet cut and aching, to a frothy inlet from the sea. Sinking onto grass under a tree, she stared for a long time at the water. It looked peaceful. Would it be warm? Anything seemed warmer than she now felt.

"Haruo," she whispered. "I am so sorry."

Rising slowly, she stood. The water would surely sooth her aching feet. Dear Joumi, he need never know. She waded out farther and farther glad of the chill that matched her broken heart.

Thirteen

Joumi caught the earliest ferry back to the mainland. The sea gleamed blue and pink beneath a spectacular sunrise. They passed the tall red Temple Gate, but this time Joumi had no desire to prostrate himself. He was going directly to find Amaya. Since it was so early, he had every hope she would be at home.

The ferry took an age to dock, slowing down, and dropping its ramps onto a concrete wharf. Once the crew opened the exit gate, since he'd crossed as a passenger, he was able to stride off the vessel fairly quickly and fetch his car. When he got to the neighborhood where Junko's cousins lived, he ran a comb through his hair and wished he'd put on fresh clothes, but no matter, he soon parked in front of the house.

The entrance led through an archway of flowering shrubs. It smelled fragrant. His hand trembled as he tapped on the front door. Through the glass he could see the movement of someone coming to answer. The door slid open and a very pretty Korean woman, almost as tall as he, looked at him curiously. "May I help you," she asked.

"I hope so," Joumi replied with a pleasant smile and a small bow of greeting. "My name is Joumi Kouki. I am a friend of Amaya's. Is she here?" The word *friend*, no sooner out of his mouth, made his face flush. He noticed the lady's slight smile and wondered if she knew about him.

"Please come in." She stepped aside. He followed her into a small sitting room. "If you'd be so kind as to wait here, I will see if she is up yet. Quite often, she likes to sleep in."

He sat on a wooden chair, his knee anxiously bouncing up and down. Was he expected, he wondered? Footsteps sounded. The door slid open and a Korean man wearing a white lab coat came in, smiling. "Mr. Kouki," he said. "I am Bae Sangh, Junko's relative. Amaya is going to be delighted you are here."

Joumi shook Bae's hand. "I hope she will be pleased," he muttered. "You knew I was coming?"

"No, Joumi, but my wife, Sonja, and I hoped Junko's letter brought good news…"

Sonja glided into the room, a worried expression on her face. "Bae, she's not in her room. She must have slipped out early before we got up."

"She probably went for a walk," Bae said amiably.

But Joumi felt his stomach lurch. "She does not like walking," he stated, remembering the time when she'd trekked a mile to chase him down on the movie set. She'd been wearing sandals that had made her feet sore. And he'd never seen her with any shoes that looked even slightly practical.

Bae and Sonja exchanged glances. "She will probably be back soon to bathe and get ready. This afternoon she is to perform at the Peace Tree ceremony."

"What time?" Joumi said, his voice demanding, his eyes troubled.

"It's at two o'clock, I believe," Sonja said in a soothing voice but her eyes showed she too was worried.

"Where else might she have gone?" Joumi's voice was now conciliatory. These people meant no harm and he needed their help.

"Often, she accompanies me to the hospital." Bae's serious face gave nothing of his emotion away. "Perhaps she went early. She loves to play her shamisen for the children and she may have wanted to practice for this afternoon."

Sonja drew in a sharp breath. "Her shamisen is in her room. I don't like to speculate, but she did not even wear shoes…"

"Then she couldn't have gone far," Joumi cried, but then he remembered Sonja saying Amaya slipped out before they got out of bed at dawn. He groaned and covered his forehead with his hands, trying to make sense of this. "I am going to look for her," he said, and hurried out the door.

~ * ~

The chant *Namu Amida Butsu, Namu Amida Butsu* sounded low in Amaya's water-logged ears. At first Amaya thought her name was being called and she managed to search the uneven waters of the sea. She glimpsed a small boat. A wave swept over her head and for a moment she gasped for breath. Salt stung her eyes and her mouth. Her body, already chilled, was losing its strength, but somehow she found herself fighting to hold on to life, but she told herself to be brave, to let go, to plunge beneath the surface. To find peace.

A fishing skiff drew up close to her thrashing body. Strong arms reached down into the surf, and she was fished out of the water. Hardly conscious, she vaguely heard a deep voice telling her to not give up. "Missy," the fisherman said, wrapping her in a woolen coat and rubbing her arms, her legs, her feet. "Do not throw away your life. Nothing is so bad as that. Nothing. Call upon the name of *Amida*. He will forgive your past transgressions. You will enter the Pure Land, but not yet. You are too young to die."

Amaya blacked out and awoke to find herself in a clean hospital bed. She stared at the bare ceiling, glad to be alive, but ashamed to have failed.

A nurse stepped up to the bed. "So, you are awake." She took Amaya's wrist. "Your pulse is normal. I will call Dr. Sangh and let him know. He was most worried about you." She walked briskly out of view.

Amaya shrank under the sheet. What could she tell Bae and Sonja after all their kindness to her? Now she brought shame upon them, and everyone in this hospital must know what she'd tried to do. She heard Bae enter the room and felt his presence standing over her, silently watching her. He had every right to be angry.

~ * ~

Joumi drove frantically up and down the back streets and alleys. Finally, he abandoned his car in a cul-de-sac and went on foot, running down a narrow gravel path, shouting, "Amaya, Amaya answer me. Where are you?" In agony he came to the inlet from the sea and stared out at the frothy water. The mountains seemed to swallow the waterway. A couple of fishing boats had dropped their nets and bobbed up and down. He wanted to hail the crew but his voice stuck in his throat. If they'd seen her, they would not be calmly fishing. Yes, he told himself. Perhaps she has already gone back to the doctor's house. He ran all the way back to arrive gasping on their doorstep.

Sonja ushered him into the house, sitting him in a comfortable chair, and gently wiping his forehead.

"Be patient," she said. "She will come home. You'll see. I will bring you tea and you must eat something."

Joumi heard someone coming into the house, but Sonja dashed his hopes. "That sounds like Bae." Then she gave him back his hope. "He never comes home so early. Perhaps he has news."

Joumi jumped to his feet staring at the doorway and immediately engaging the doctor's attention.

Bae nodded. "She is all right," he said without ceremony. "She almost drowned but we have her in the hospital under observation. A fisherman picked her up and brought her in."

Joumi, already striding towards the door, hardly heard the good doctor's words.

"Wait," Bae said. "You must ride back to the hospital with me."

~ * ~

Amaya could hear the breathing above her head and kept her eyes firmly closed. "I am so sorry, Bae," she said, pulling the sheet down to her chin, uncovering her eyes but unwilling to open them. "I have caused you so much trouble."

"No, my darling. It is I who am sorry. It is all my fault. I should never have let you out of my sight for a moment." Joumi bent and gently kissed her cheek. "We should already be married."

Amaya's eyes flashed open. She wanted to escape. Joumi's gentle look calmed her.

"I will never hurt you," Joumi said. "I want to take care of you, but only if it is what you wish."

Amaya began to weep, unable to say it was what she wished, had always been what she wished, but now it was spoiled forever because she was soiled goods, ruined, not a woman any man could ever want for long, and certainly not good enough for Joumi.

Joumi sat on the side of the bed and stroked her hair away from her eyes. "I am not good enough for you."

"You," she whispered. "Not you. I have done unspeakable things."

"You are not alone," he replied. "Let us not talk of what is past. I want to marry you."

Surely he could not realize how unfit she was to be anyone's wife. "You don't understand."

"Nothing you have done can change how I feel about you." Joumi smiled and reached his face to hers, kissing her mouth. "I have longed to do that," he said.

Amaya lay there frozen, afraid. She did not want sex with any man again, but this man, this Joumi, his lips had set her on fire.

"My darling," he said, and kissed her again slowly, stroking her face, cupping her breasts, kissing her shoulders.

She put her arms around him and drew him onto the bed. "Wait," he groaned, went quickly to the door, handed an orderly some money. "Please keep everyone outside."

Soon, he lay next to her on the bed, holding her.

Once again she felt herself become frigid with fright.

"We need do nothing you do not wish," he said, stroking her stomach, touching her thighs so that she began to tingle with longing.

Their eyes met and held in a long, deep gaze. He felt as if he could see into her soul, and what he saw took his breath away. She was a wounded, frightened fawn, but she was also a she-bear full of strength and grace. "I love you," he murmured.

Amaya gazed deeply into Joumi's eyes aware of how often she'd played a game of sexual pretense with men, but this time, she was not playing. She was too weak and too broken to pretend untruths, and she wanted this man like she'd never wanted anyone. "You don't know me," she muttered.

He kissed her into silence.

Afterword

They consummated their relationship in that hospital bed and though Joumi begged Amaya to marry him, she never would. They lived together happily, but she refused to move back to Tokyo, preferring to stay in her hometown where she became a nurse so she could take care of the sick and needy who'd suffered so much.

Joumi became a very rich man and built her a castle on a mountain where they could sit on their patio and watch the sea crashing against the mountains.

Thus they spent several years of bliss.

Amaya contracted tuberculosis. The day she began coughing up blood, Joumi wanted to send her to the best doctors in the world but she would not go.

On June 4th, 1960, she smiled up at Joumi who had carried her out to their patio above the sea. "They are here," she said, seeing invisible ghosts.

"I know." Joumi could hardly believe how light she had become, herself almost a ghost.

"I love you," she whispered, and expired in his arms.

After her funeral, attended by many from the hospital, including Bae and Sonja, and also Junko, he saw a lawyer. He donated some money to the Kabuki Theater in Tokyo, he made Junko a rich woman, he set Ginza Girl up in a dress shop, and the rest he left to the hospital for those who needed lifelong care and could not pay. He considered throwing himself into the sea to be with his beloved, but instead he decided he, like Amaya, would dedicate the rest of his life to helping others.

On June 4th, 1961, exactly one year after Amaya's death, he entered a Jodo Shu Monastery where he eventually became a Pure Land monk.

The End

About the Author

Christina St Clair, born and raised in England, has lived in France and Germany, but now resides in the United States where she has been a chemist, a pastor, a spiritual director, and a novelist. She is interested in multiculturism and the spirituality of many traditions, including Buddhism. Ten Yen is the prequel to a series which includes Ten Yen True (co-authored with Amanda Armstrong), Ten Yen Forever (Amanda Armstrong), with another story in the works.

Also by Christina St. Clair
at
Rogue Phoenix Press

Ten Yen True
With Amanda Armstrong

Kaizen! That's what Caitlin, JJ, Paul, and Tommy need—to change for the better. When they each mysteriously receive one of four ten yen coins, none of them know or understand why or where their journey is about to take them.

Ten Yen True intertwines the lives of four people, all of whom have need of one another to bring about healing and wholeness and are being mysteriously helped by a Japanese monk. It is a story of hope, love, forgiveness and miracles, exploring the spiritual and psychological underpinnings of the main characters, demonstrating the interconnectedness of human beings.

Unexpected Journey

Unexpected Journey is a historical novel set in England and colonial America in the 1730s.

A wide gulf existed between people from different social strata. Lenape natives in Pennsylvania felt no love for white people who'd forced them from their land. Rich English girls had no interest in brown-skinned natives in the colonies and certainly did not expect to meet any. Street girls eked out an existence any way they could, with no hope of fraternizing with the wealthy. Yet Gishuk, Rachel, and Anna are just such people—thrown together in a tale of adventure, friendship, and danger.

VISIT OUR WEBSITE
FOR THE FULL INVENTORY
OF QUALITY BOOKS:

http://www.roguephoenixpress.com

Rogue Phoenix Press

Representing Excellence in Publishing

*Quality trade paperbacks and downloads
in multiple formats,
in genres ranging from historical to
contemporary romance, mystery and science
fiction.
Visit the website then bookmark it.
We add new titles each month!*